The King's Champion

M. H. Bonham

WOLFSINGER

PUBLICATIONS

Wolfsinger Publications Security, Colorado

ACKNOWLEDGEMENTS

A special thanks goes to the following people:

Carol Hightshoe, friend and publisher, for taking this project on.
Selina Rosen and Lynn Stranathan of Yard Dog Press who
introduced readers to Kalena and Romarin.
Matthew Wayne Selnick, my first reader who has also written
Brave Men Run, who graciously blurbed the cover.
And my husband, Larry, who acts as editor.

A special acknowledgment goes to a particular white Alaskan
Malamute who is the inspiration for Othala.

Cover art copyright © 2008 by Lee Kuruganti
Published using
Lulu.com
3131 RDU Center, Suite 210
Morrisville, NC 27560

ISBN 978-0-6152-1674-4
Printed and bound in the United States of America

Dedication

To Larry, as always.

And to my furry muses, Kira, Kodiak, Haegl, Mishka and Hailey for inspiration.

Chapter One

A loud screech, like that of an angry hawk, resounded off the parapets of Citadel Heights. Kalena hesitated in her practice and looked up, her skin prickling in cold fear. She wanted to run – to hide anywhere she could. And yet, she knew there was no place that was safe. Another screech. It was so loud that she expected to see a dark shadow flying over her at any moment.

"Steady, Kally," said Cahal. The old *Chi'lan* warrior grinned at her reassuringly. He was tall *Chi'lan* with the characteristic red-gold hair and silver eyes that marked both him and Kalena as being from the *Lochvaur* kindred. But while Kalena was young – a swordbearer *chi'li'a* and not a full *Chi'lan* warrior – Cahal was older and seasoned with numerous battle scars. "They die from the sword as we do."

Kalena blinked and swallowed, not realizing she had held her breath. "I'm sorry, Champion," she said, lowering her broadsword. "I wish I knew how to control the fear."

Cahal smiled. "We all have fear, Kally. As a *Chi'lan*, you learn to control it." He shaded his eyes with his hands. "I'm surprised the watchtowers haven't called alarm. I felt that screech in my bones."

Kalena chuckled, despite her fear. "I'll go inside to help the garrison prepare..."

"No," Cahal said. "I want you to stand with me."

Kalena stared. "With you, Champion? But I'm a *chi'li'a*..."

"Soon to be *Chi'lan*. Don't you think it's time you saw battle, instead of staying behind the lines?"

Kalena's throat tightened, and she could hear her heart pounding in her ears with excitement. She nodded and stood in ready stance next to Cahal, her sword drawn. Cahal shielded his eyes once more against the afternoon sun, his own sword, the legendary *Fyren* in his right hand. Kalena glanced at the long sword – its silver adamantine blade held a dark stain across it as though blood had permanently etched itself in the metal.

Another screech and Kalena fought the urge to cover her ears. *Where was the damn watch? Chi'lan* warriors were already pouring out of the garrison.

"Fireworm!" the watch called out.

Kalena gazed into deep blue sky, looking for movement. Yet, all she saw were the massive gray stone of the Shadow Mountains. She turned to look at the cliffs on the north face of Citadel Heights. The fortress city, built along the ridge, was impervious to any ground-based attacks, but against air assault, it was as vulnerable as any other.

Then, Kalena saw a dark speck along the gray cliffs. She hadn't seen the worm because it was so well camouflaged against the rocks behind it. It was thirty feet long – a mature fireworm – with black scales and a thin, serpent-like body. It watched the fortress with glittering obsidian eyes and opened its mouth to hiss at them, exposing the large, sharp teeth. It writhed like a serpent in the air.

"There it is!" she shouted, pointing to the upper ridge.

"Good eyes," Cahal said brusquely. "The Heights!" he shouted to those manning the siege engines. "Turn the ballistas!" Others took up the cry and the soldiers scrambled to turn the heavy siege weapons. Cahal tugged at her sleeve. "Come on – we'll have a fight on the curtain wall. It'll come to us." He led her out of the courtyard and up the steps that led to the wall walk.

"Where are the others?" she asked breathlessly as they ran up the stairs.

"The other *Chi'lan*?" Cahal asked. He pointed to the warriors already on the wall walk. "Lochalan is leading them."

"No, the other worms – they seldom attack alone," she said.

Cahal frowned. "You're right." A group of about twenty five warriors had gathered, many Kalena knew. Among them was Lochalan, her older brother, and another *Chi'lan* named Falar, who was the first *Chi'lan* from the *Redel* kindred she had ever seen. "I want you to spread out along the wall walk but keep close enough so we can cover each other."

There was a murmur of assent and *Chi'lan* dispersed. Lochalan and Falar approached.

"What are you doing here, Kally?" said Lochalan.

Falar frowned, looking at the insignia on her surcoat. "You're *chi'li'a*, you're not allowed here."

"She's with me," Cahal said before Kalena could speak. "She's testing for *Chi'lan* next week."

Kalena almost gasped. *So soon?* she wondered. She had only been apprenticed for five years. That would make her the youngest *Chi'lan* since King Romarin, himself. She met Cahal's gaze. The old *Chi'lan's* eyes glittered, confirming his words.

"You've deserved it – I haven't seen such talent in years." Cahal turned to the others. "Get ready! We've got a worm to fight."

The fireworm hissed and flapped its wings. Kalena watched it, fascinated and repulsed by the odd movements. As much as she hated them, she had to admit they were beautiful in their own deadly way.

Suddenly, the fireworm screamed. Its undulating body straightened and it shot directly for them. Kalena yelled and raised her sword in time to parry the fireworm's claws as it attacked.

Cahal was faster. His long sword cleaved the creature's neck. Black blood spewed everywhere, and the worm collapsed, thrashing in its final death throes.

Kalena stared at Cahal's sword. "Thank you…" she stammered, meeting the commander's gaze.

"No time for that, Kally, look!"

She turned to see two more fireworms attack *Chi'lan* fifty feet from them. The two *Chi'lan* who met the assault were none other than Falar and her brother, Lochalan. Kalena yelled and charged, swinging her broadsword as a fireworm broke through Falar's defenses and raked the *Chi'lan* with its venomous talons. Falar's sword had cut into the creature's hide, but had caught between the hardened scales and he was struggling to pull it away. The fireworm lashed out, its teeth coming down on his head, only to glance off the helm. But the impact was enough to stun Falar and he collapsed. The fireworm grasped the hapless warrior in its claws, preparing to take off.

Kalena slammed her sword into the beast, cutting just above the shoulder. The blade sliced deep, tearing into connective tissue and neck. The fireworm screamed and whipped its head around, but Kalena was already moving. It shot a blast of flames at her and her cloak and surcoat caught fire.

She dropped to the ground and rolled. From somewhere, she heard her brother scream her name. The fireworm went after her, leaving Falar. She felt the massive claws bat at her like a cat plays with a mouse, but her armor held. Kalena leapt up to see nothing but coils and shoved her sword upward with all her strength.

A deafening screech and her sword was wrenched from her hands. The fireworm slammed against her and she was thrown once more to the ground. The beast slammed into her once, twice, and then, thrashed terribly. Her vision became dim and unfocused. Then, she felt someone grip her and drag her away.

Chapter Two

"Kally! Kally!" her brother's voice rang in her ears. "You all right?"

Kalena couldn't speak. All she could do was watch the creature flounder in its final death throes. She felt sick to her stomach and so wobbly that if she were forced to stand, she was certain she would pass out or throw up. She hurt everywhere; she wondered how bad the worm had cooked her. Someone pressed water against her lips and splashed the cold water against her face. She gripped the flask and drank. She hadn't even realized how much her throat burned until now.

"Is she all right?" Cahal's voice came from behind her.

"I'm not sure – she isn't moving much," Lochalan said.

"Fa-fa.." she stammered and stopped. It hurt too much to talk.

"He's badly wounded, but the healers are tending to him," Lochalan said. "You saved him, Kally."

"Not bad for a *chi'li'a*?" Cahal knelt beside her. To her shock, he was covered with blood and soot. She tried to touch the wound on his face. "Don't worry about me. Did you get any venom into you?"

Kalena blinked. She hurt a lot but she didn't remember the claws actually puncturing her mail. *Fireworm venom burns at the wound*, she remembered Cahal telling her. She shook her head. "The worms?" Her voice came out in a hoarse croak.

"Gone – you killed the last of them," Lochalan said.

"They'll be back," Cahal said. "This was just a test."

"Anyone dead?"

"Several wounded," Lochalan said. "We were lucky. Can you stand?"

Kalena wasn't in the mood to stand but gritted her teeth and nodded. She didn't want to appear weak. She accepted her brother's strong arm as he helped her to her feet. To her chagrin, her knees tried to buckle under her.

Cahal caught her left arm and slung it over his shoulder. "Let's get you to the infirmary," he said. "The healers can take care of you there."

"I'm fine," she protested.

"No, you're not," the champion said. "You have some nasty burns that need tending to."

She let them lead her to the infirmary. Thankfully, both men let her try to walk rather than humiliating her by carrying her in their arms. The infirmary was a makeshift hospital that had been a guardroom at one time, but had been converted many years before due to the fireworm attacks. The room was filled with injured soldiers – most with cuts and bruises. A few were being treated for bad burns.

A group of healers were gathered around two men. Kalena glanced at Lochalan, whose expression was grim. "Who is it?" Kalena asked.

"Falar and Sillanen," Lochalan said. "Sillanen caught the brunt of the fireworm's flames when it went down..."

"Then, it was my fault..." Kalena said. Her throat tightened.

"No, Kally, she was in the wrong place at the wrong time," Cahal said. "No one is blaming you. You're a hero – if you hadn't attacked, Falar would be dead." He glanced at Lochalan. "Let's get her to a cot."

"I'm fine," she protested but to no avail. They walked her over to the bunk and she sat down.

"I'll find a healer," said Cahal. "You stay here."

Kalena watched as Cahal walked towards the group of healers.

Lochalan turned to her. "Kally, that was a dangerous thing you did today..."

But Kalena wasn't listening. She was watching Cahal who had approached the group of healers. They parted just a bit, and for a moment, Kalena caught a glimpse of a *Lochvaur* who was sitting beside Falar. She stared at his face – she felt as if she should know him from somewhere. He wore the mail and surcoat of a *Chi'lan* and yet, she didn't recall him. There weren't many *Lochvaur* left and fewer still who were *Chi'lan*. The fireworms had all but decimated the *Lochvaur* kindred.

The *Lochvaur*, like all *Eleion*, were exceedingly long lived. Some, like Cahal, had lived for hundreds of years, but most of the warriors were younger than a couple hundred and most were like Kalena, not even past a century. Battle with enemies and fireworms over the years had ravaged the *Chi'lan* warriors.

Cahal turned to the warrior who sat next to Falar. Although she couldn't hear what they were saying, she could tell by Cahal's demeanor that they were friends. The warrior turned to Falar and laid his hands on the man. One hand was bare, but a silver gauntlet covered the other. Falar cried out as a blue light emanated from the warrior's hands...

"Who is that?" Kalena said, interrupting her brother.

Lochalan frowned. "You mean Falar?"

"No, the *Lochvaur*."

"You mean the king?"

Kalena caught her breath. "That's Romarin Nevfaras?" As *chi'li'a*, she had seen the king, but only from a distance. As *Chi'lan*, she would serve him as one of his elite warriors.

"Kally, you haven't been listening to me," Lochalan said.

"No, I haven't," she agreed. "He really does have a silver hand, doesn't he? Why is he here?"

"He's first-blood," Lochalan said. "He's the son of Rhyn'athel."

"Son of the warrior god?" Kalena stared. "Then the rumors are true." She watched as Falar's writhing diminished and he started breathing normally again. The light faded from Romarin's hands and he slumped backwards in the chair.

Kalena glanced at her brother, who had also fallen silent while watching the healing. "What about Sillanen?" She could see the woman's charred body now as the king slowly stood up and walked away. Cahal spoke to the king again and Romarin patted the champion on the back before leaving. The healers covered her body.

Lochalan shook his head. "She may have been too far gone. Some wounds are even beyond a first-blood to heal."

Kalena lowered her head. "I should've been more careful."

"You did the best you could," said Cahal. She looked up and saw a man, obviously a healer, standing beside Cahal. But unlike Cahal, her brother, and herself, this man was not pureblooded *Eleion* as they were. His eyes were a mottled color and his silver hair was streaked with brown.

"Hello, Kalena, my name is Daimhan." The man sat beside her. "Yes, I'm *Shara'kai*. I'm also a healer."

She nodded. A *Shara'kai* was a half-blood – one from both the *Eleion* and Ansgar races. She knew some *Eleion* were loathed to deal with them, but Kalena was pragmatic. Romarin had let a few of the *Shara'kai* become *Chi'lan* – they had become some of the best warriors. "I think I'm all right," she said. "Just beaten up a bit."

"I'll be the judge of that," said Daimhan. He glanced at Lochalan. "Can you help me with her mail?"

They stripped off the burnt surcoat and the mail. Kalena groaned as they pulled the hauberk off her arms and began unfastening the arming jacket.

Daimhan touched her hair. "You singed your hair pretty bad, *chi'li'a*, you'll need to cut it off."

"She'll be cropping it," said Cahal. "Next week she makes *Chi'lan.*"

"Well, if Cahal trained you, I'm not surprised you're making *Chi'lan* so young," Daimhan said.

Stripped of the arming jacket and mail. Kalena felt naked in just a tunic and breeches. Her clothing had just a few scorch marks but showed no other problems. Daimhan checked her arms and shoulders, rotating each one carefully.

"Oww!" Kalena jumped as he moved her right arm upward.

"Hmm, bad strain," Daimhan said. He looked up at Cahal. "You're prized pupil was very, very lucky." He touched her shoulder and she winced. He looked underneath at the back of her neck. "Hmmm, some redness – light burns really. You are lucky you didn't get cooked. Your cloak, surcoat and gambeson took the brunt of the flames."

"She rolled," Lochalan said.

"Good thinking," Daimhan said. "Does anything else hurt?"

She shook her head. "Just feel bruised up."

Daimhan nodded. "I'm going to leave you with some salve for the burns – it'll work on any nicks and cuts too as long as they're not too deep. I recommend resting for a day or two and then light workouts. After that, you can fight fireworms again."

"If it's all the same to you, I think I'd rather not," she said weakly. "Can I go back to the barracks?"

Daimhan glanced at Cahal. "I'd rather you didn't. *Chi'lan* have a nasty tendency of pushing themselves when they should be resting. Unless there's more attacks, I'd rather have you here."

Cahal nodded. "You'll stay here until Daimhan says you should leave."

"Yes, sir." She tried not to sound disappointed but she knew better than to argue with the champion. She gingerly sat back on the cot.

"Well, if you will excuse me, I have wounded to attend to," Daimhan said with a nod and left.

"Don't worry; I'm sure Daimhan will throw you out in a couple of days." Cahal winked. He became serious once more. "When you're released, come see me. We'll get you ready for the *Chi'lan* trials."

Kalena nodded and watched the champion leave. The sun had dropped behind the mountains to the west and cast the room into shadows. The flurry of activity that had come with the new patients from the fireworm attacks now subsided as patients were being attended to. Lochalan waited for Cahal to go before turning to her. "Kally, what you did today was dangerous."

Kalena blinked and met her brother's earnest gaze. "Lochalan, Cahal says I'm ready."

"That's not it," Lochalan said. He looked down at the floor and then back at her. "I don't know exactly how to put it."

"What?"

"I'm worried about you."

Kalena began to laugh and then saw he was serious. "Why? I'm training to be *Chi'lan* just like you and our parents..."

"That's just it, Kally, we come from a long line of warriors." He paused and took her hand. "I was hoping you – of all of us – might choose a different path."

"What do you mean?"

"Not be *Chi'lan*."

Kalena almost laughed and stopped when she looked into his silver eyes. "You're serious."

"Quite serious," Lochalan said. "Kally, we're the last of our family – our bloodline. Our parents died fighting these stupid worms and most likely, I will die fighting them. You still have a choice – you haven't taken Rhyn'athel's oath. You can leave the way of the warrior while you still can. No one will think ill of you."

"And what do I do?" she asked.

"There's the court. We're *Lochvaur*, which makes us the closest thing to nobility. You could find a husband, settle down..."

Kalena stared at him. "Are you crazy? You're asking me to be a court lady?" She could see Lochalan's concern in his eyes. *He truly believes he isn't going to live much longer.*

He hesitated and shook his head. "I don't know, Kally. I just became scared today, that's all. Seeing you fighting that fireworm terrified me. I realized you're the only family I have." He stood up and paced. "It's bad enough I nearly lost Falar." He glanced over at the *Redel* who was lying quietly. "I know they tell you when you become *Chi'lan* to never become too attached to anyone. That you could lose a friend in an instant. And yet, Kally, we have nothing else but each other. That and our families. And soon, I may not even have that."

Kalena gripped her brother's hand. "Lochalan, what the Web of Wyrd spins is not ours to guess. I have always wanted to be *Chi'lan*, nothing more."

Lochalan shook his head. "I know, Kally, but I'm asking you to reconsider. Rhyn'athel is demanding of his warriors – I have seen many good men and women die for this god. I don't want you to be one of them."

"Cahal says I'm the most talented *Chi'lan* he's seen in a long time. I was born to be a *Chi'lan*, Lochalan, can't you see?"

Lochalan's frown deepened. "Kally, I can't let you throw away your life like this. As your older brother, I'm in charge…"

"What are you saying?" She turned pale. "I'm of age. I've been of age for five years now."

"Yes, but I can still invoke familial right."

"You wouldn't dare. Cahal won't hear of it."

"I'm going to Romarin with it if I have to." With that, he stalked off.

Chapter Three

Romarin Nevfaras, the son of Rhyn'athel, the warrior god, stared into the sky from the small window in the throne room. The sun had already set on Citadel Heights and the stars were beginning to wink into the twilight sky. He had lost one good *Chi'lan* today and nearly lost another had it not been for a *chi'li'a*. Sillanen had been a good warrior and had fought for Romarin for almost twenty years. Romarin's silver hand curled into a fist. The pain of losing a warrior, who would've given her life for him, left him feeling angry and empty. He felt helpless. In all the time he had been her king and commander, he realized he hadn't really known her. He knew Sillanen was good with a sword, though better with a bow, beating nearly every *Chi'lan* in competition. But beyond that, she had been almost a nameless face.

And yet, the anger and pain came from something much deeper. The black dragon mark of Rhyn'athel was still on his forearm just above the gauntlet, marking him as Rhyn'athel's Champion, and no one would argue that he was the warrior god's son, but alone he could do nothing against the onslaught of fireworms. Each attack wore them down; each time he dreaded possibly losing another warrior to the creatures. The *Chi'lan* were dwindling – endangered of disappearing forever.

He had to console himself that *Chi'lan* Falar was still alive. Being a godling gave Romarin the power to heal wounds, but not the power to snatch the dead away from the death god. Like everything in his life, Romarin had to make a choice. Sillanen was too close to Areyn's realm for Romarin to try to bring her back – not with Falar clinging to life. Areyn had won Sillanen; Romarin decided he would be damned if the death god took Falar too. It had been a struggle nonetheless but Romarin had his small victory. Falar had been Lochalan's *chi'li'a* who had made *Chi'lan* a few years before.

The pyre for Sillanen would be lit tonight. He would stand there and watch as flames consumed the body. *As Rhyn'athel brought us forth from the fire of Creation and Destruction, so we must return.*

Romarin's mind turned to the *chi'li'a* who had saved Falar. He had seen her fight along the wall walk. She *was* impressive. Normally, Romarin would not have let an apprentice warrior fight alongside his hardened warriors, but Cahal had convinced him that it was time for the *chi'li'a* to prove herself. It appeared she had.

"I was right, wasn't I?" Cahal said.

Romarin smiled as he turned. He had known Cahal all his life; having trained under Cahal when he was boy. Cahal was very old for an *Eleion* – so old, he actually remembered not only Romarin's mother, but also her parents and theirs as well. In fact, Cahal had fought beside the warrior god, himself, nearly 1500 years before in the *Athel'cen* War. Cahal had known the greatest *Eleion* warrior, Lachlan Ah'rhyn and his brother, Elsonre. The same warrior whom Romarin was assumed to be the current incarnation of. Indeed, Romarin sometimes had a feeling that he had known Cahal in a past life. Some of Cahal's mannerisms or speech would invoke long-forgotten memories that Romarin never had.

"Yes, you were," he said. "What was her name again?"

"Kalena," Cahal said. "She's Lochalan's sister."

"Lochalan?" Romarin said. "She fights nothing like him."

"No, she doesn't," said Cahal. "She's better. I didn't believe it myself until Reneyl showed her to me. She had surpassed his ability in a fight."

"Reneyl?" Romarin said, raising his eyebrows. "She bested him?"

"Yes – I've had her up against other *Chi'lan* too."

"Is she first-blood?"

"No," said Cahal, "but she comes out of warrior lines nonetheless. Her line hails from Tamar."

"Tamar was a great warrior," Romarin mused. "Perhaps she inherited some of her fighting ability from him."

"Or perhaps she is a great warrior in her own right," Cahal said. "There are those who became great not out of bloodlines but out of their own ability."

Romarin chuckled. "Indeed." Cahal was one such warrior. "So tell me about this Kalena."

"She's the best warrior I've seen since Lachlan," he said. Romarin raised his eyebrow but made no reply. "Yes, she's better than you," Cahal added. "She's lightning quick with a sword. It's little wonder she's ready for the Trials."

"No."

Romarin and Cahal turned to see Lochalan stride in. The younger *Chi'lan*'s gaze glinted with anger. "I'm invoking my familial rights. Kalena must not become *Chi'lan*," Lochalan said.

"Familial right?" Cahal repeated. "Kally is of age – she can make her own decision."

"Kally is the last of my family," Lochalan said. "I am the head of my family and invoke familial right to decide if she should become *Chi'lan*."

Romarin frowned. "*Chi'li'a* Kalena saved Falar. Why shouldn't she become *Chi'lan*?"

Lochalan's face became unreadable. "I won't permit her to undergo the Trials."

"And I, as the King's Champion and commander of the *Chi'lan* say she does," Cahal said.

"Familial law trumps your word."

Cahal glanced at Lochalan and then at Romarin. "We shall see, *Chi'lan*. If anyone has the final say, it would be the king."

Both turned to Romarin. Romarin frowned. He had not expected this.

"Kalena is ready to be *Chi'lan*. She saved Falar – she deserves the chance to be what she has trained to be," Cahal said.

Romarin turned to Lochalan. "And what is your argument, Lochalan? She saved Falar from certain death."

"And nearly got herself killed," Lochalan said. He paused and looked down at his feet. "My king, I know what I say makes little sense and perhaps I speak more with my heart than with reason. Kalena is the last of my family's line. We come from a very old line of *Chi'lan* who have served the *Lochvaur* kings even before Lachlei. I have chosen the *Chi'lan* way and I do not regret my choice. But with the peril we all face, it is unlikely that I will see a son or daughter to carry on that tradition. Kalena is young and there are many here who would consider marrying her..." His voice trailed off as he met Cahal's glare.

"Don't you think that should be her choice?" Cahal said. "We don't marry off our women like chattel the way the *Redel* or *Lochel* did."

"No one says she can't marry once she becomes *Chi'lan*," Romarin said.

"But most do not," Lochalan said. "Look at your warriors – how many have married and how many of those have children?"

"It's *their* choice," Cahal said.

"And it is my choice that my sister doesn't get locked into a decision she can't change. Once she's a *Chi'lan*, she is always one. Rhyn'athel's vow is not one taken lightly."

A silence ensued and they both looked at Romarin. The king shook his head. "I don't think this is a decision for either of you. The person who needs to be here is Kalena, herself." He paused as he noted Cahal's triumphant expression. "I haven't made up my mind, old friend. She may be good, but Lochalan does have a point. We're losing our warriors at an alarming rate. The old blood is disappearing and there are fewer and fewer *Lochvaur*."

"Do you wish me to bring her?" Cahal said.

"Yes, both of you shall go," he said. He glared at them. "But say nothing of this conversation or try to persuade her, or I shall choose in the other's favor."

Chapter Four

Kalena stood at the ironbound, double doors that led into the high king's throne room. She shivered nervously, cold in the tunic and breeches she still wore from the infirmary. The healers had given her clean clothes – a blue tunic and tan breeches made from soft, sueded leather and a thick, brown leather belt that made the tunic less billowy. The clothing had been a man's but was at least clean and smelled faintly of soap.

She did not have the chance to cut her singed hair when Cahal and Lochalan appeared. They had said little to her except that the king wanted to see her. She could tell the two had been arguing, probably about her, given Lochalan's involvement, but when she asked further, neither man was willing to speak. They left her here before the throne room's imposing doors.

It was important – it had to be, given the time of night. The *Chi'lan* and their *chi'li'a* would be in mead hall eating dinner. Kalena was hungry, having snatched only a slice of bread and an apple before heading to speak to the king. Cahal told her he would have the kitchen save her some dinner. She hoped he would.

A guard swung the door open and motioned her inside. The room looked dark and foreboding, lit only with the smoky sconces and oil lamps. Kalena had never been in the throne room and paused. Being a *chi'li'a* did not prepare one for court etiquette and she felt small and terrified. What if she did something wrong? What if she offended the king? She did not even know if she should bow or curtsey. And did she curtsey if she was a warrior? And how would she address him?

"Come in, *chi'li'a* Kalena," Romarin's voice boomed from inside.

She tentatively stepped in, and was at once overwhelmed. The smoky room was huge with benches and tables large enough to seat hundreds of warriors. Along the walls were tapestries of *Chi'lan* warriors fighting in heroic battles. One was of a warrior with a glowing sword, leading *Chi'lan* into a charge. She stared at it in awe – she had never seen so many *Lochvaur* as depicted.

"It is impressive, isn't it?" Romarin said.

Kalena turned to see the king standing right beside her. He was a handsome *Lochvaur*. Standing beside her, he was even more impressive than when she had seen him in the infirmary. He was easily six inches taller than she – and she was not short – and held a presence that she had felt with Cahal, only more so. Her eyes went wide and her throat dried up. Her mouth moved, but no sound came out. She felt shaky. *This is really a son of Rhyn'athel*, she thought.

Romarin smiled at her. "You know, I was never comfortable with court either," he said. "It took me years to relax."

"Really?" she asked, her voice sounding squeaky. *Like a frightened mouse*, she thought. "I would've thought you'd been used to it."

Romarin shook his head. "Cahal helped me quite a bit after Krysa died. He's had plenty of experience being a surrogate father, I guess." He chuckled at what she guessed was an inside joke. He paused and smiled. "You don't remember your parents, do you?"

Kalena shook her head. "I was maybe a year when they died."

"I remember Feolan and Silanyn," Romarin said. "They were good *Chi'lan* – some of the best warriors I've known. Your brother had just made *Chi'lan* before they were killed. He was Cahal's *chi'li'a*."

Kalena nodded. "Cahal says he was good."

"Cahal says you're better."

Silence ensued. Kalena shrugged and noted that Romarin was appraising her. She knew she did not look like much – she was a bit on the scrawny side, if anything. "I do all right in a fight."

"Cahal says you're as good as another warrior from long ago." His eyes turned to the *Lochvaur* warrior with the glowing sword.

Kalena's eyes followed his gaze. "Who is that?"

"Who do you think he is?"

"Lachlan Ah'rhyn? Son of Rhyn'athel?" She laughed. "I don't think I'm that good."

Romarin smiled. "Indulge me for a moment and let's say you are that good."

"All right," she said uneasily. She did not know where the king was going with this.

"Your brother, Lochalan, is claiming familial right and demands that you should not be *Chi'lan*."

"I am twenty years old," she said. "I have been of age for five years."

"I know, and had not you bested Reneyl, you may still be apprenticed." Romarin frowned. "What do you want to do, *chi'li'a* Kalena?"

"Become *Chi'lan*, of course."

"Are you sure?" Romarin looked hard at her and Kalena flinched. She had the feeling he could see deep within her mind – the feeling was unpleasant. Yet as quickly as the feeling happened, it disappeared. To her surprise, Romarin's face turned red. "I'm sorry," he said, turning away.

Kalena's gaze narrowed. She had heard of a first-blood's ability of being able to "hear" others' thoughts but had never experienced it until now. "Why don't you just ask me?" she said. "I will answer you as honestly as I can."

"You and your brother are the last of Tamar's line," Romarin said. "Lochalan knows as well as I do that if that line is lost, the *Lochvaur* will have suffered a tragedy."

"And what about the line of Cahal? Of Haellsil? Of Lachlan? Of Elsonre?" Kalena said. "What of the thousands of *Chi'lan* who are on those tapestries?" She paused. "What of the line of the son of Rhyn'athel?"

Romarin looked as if for a moment he might be angry, but then chuckled. "Cahal didn't tell me you were this bold."

"No? Well he should've," Kalena said. "What makes my line any more important than anyone else's? No one was worried when I became Reneyl's *chi'li'a*. No one spoke up when Cahal took interest in me. Only now, when I am on the verge of becoming *Chi'lan* does my brother come to you."

Romarin shook his head. "Walk with me a bit, *chi'li'a*," he said. Kalena followed Romarin out of the throne room doors and down the long hall that led towards the courtyards of the castle. He smiled at her wonderment as she walked beside him, too nervous to say anything but curious nonetheless. "I hate staying in the throne room," he confided as they walked into the courtyard. It was dark beneath the stars and they stood in the cold night's air to wait for their eyes to adjust. As hers did, she could see that the trees were bare from winter. "It threatens to make me forget who and what I really am."

Kalena shook her head but said nothing.

"What?" he asked.

"I don't understand," she said. "You are king."

"I am *Chi'lan*," Romarin said. "I was *Chi'lan* before I became king. Yes, my mother, Krysa, was queen for many years after Nevfaras, but that was not inherited. She too was *Chi'lan*. And so was Nevfaras."

"But you are the son of Rhyn'athel, the warrior god," Kalena said.

"Yes," he said. "But even Lachlan Ah'rhyn, himself, became *Chi'lan*. Cahal trained him. Like he trained me. Like he trained you." He paused and gazed into her eyes, but this time, she felt no mental push. "Cahal believes you're as good of a warrior as Lachlan was. That's quite a statement coming from him. I have never known him to exaggerate anyone's talent." He grinned. "Especially mine."

Kalena laughed, despite herself. "You wouldn't believe how hard he pushes me – not that I'm complaining, mind you. It's just, well..."

"He's Cahal. I wouldn't expect anything less," said Romarin. "He says you're ready – and I believe him. But Lochalan isn't prepared for this." He took a few steps down the path and she followed. "I wouldn't be involved except they're my two highest ranking *Chi'lan*. Normally, I would have Cahal handle this, but the *Chi'lan* are at a breaking point with these fireworm attacks." He paused. "So am I."

Kalena nodded. "Fireworms killed my parents."

"The attacks have been consistent but they were never this bad," Romarin said. "At least, as far as I know. Cahal told me they increased after Nevfaras' death. That was over a year before I was born." He paused and stopped to stare into the sky. "But lately the attacks have been worse. Much worse."

Kalena nodded. "I wonder why?"

"I've been trying to find the answer," Romarin said. "I have researched what I can and have asked Cahal and others who still remember the time before Nevfaras' death. I have come up with little save perhaps Allarun is using the fireworms against us."

"Allarun?" she shivered. "The dark lord?"

"Yes, but he has been quiescent as of late. He seemed to have been satisfied to have killed my stepfather."

Kalena nodded.

"But that does not solve the problem at hand," said Romarin. "And that is, what to do with an exceptionally talented *chi'li'a* whose brother, my captain, does not want to see made *Chi'lan*."

Kalena held her breath. Did he mean to forbid her from the Trials?

To her relief, Romarin shook his head. "Normally I would order him to accept it, but as I said, the *Chi'lan* are at a breaking point with these attacks. I can't push a high-ranking *Chi'lan* to accept something that would cause resentment and bitterness throughout my warriors. At the same time, I've seen you fight on the wall. You're impressive and I know that losing you as a warrior would be a terrible mistake."

Kalena stared at him. He sounded as though his kingship depended on her. "But, my lord, I am just a *chi'li'a...*"

"Even Cahal was just a *chi'li'a* once," he said. "Even I was. And yet there were those who saw greatness beyond the inexperience. Cahal has so much faith in you that he has brought you to my attention. I have seen something of that greatness as well." He paused. "I have come up with a solution, but it is one that will be far more difficult than you've imagined. I will allow you to enter the Trials, but..." He paused. "I will choose the three *Chi'lan* you will fight."

Kalena swallowed hard. "I am to fight *Chi'lan*, not *chi'li'a?*"

"*Chi'lan*," Romarin said. "That's how it was done in the old days or so Cahal tells me. Lachlan Ah'rhyn went against Tamar, Cahal, and Lachlei, herself. It'll be harder than simple sparring too. It's fought until one draws blood."

Kalena's throat tightened. "*carae aeli i'na var*" "*Until first blood drawn*" – she remembered the stories Cahal told her. Some *Chi'lan* and *chi'li'a* died at the Trials because the first blood drawn was sometimes the last. Even with the control of a *Chi'lan* warrior, there were still accidents.

"Nevfaras changed that," Romarin said. "We were losing too many good warriors to Allarun's wars and he preferred to have the Trials be more of a test of skill. So, he made it more of a sport and less of a battle. Cahal has thought in doing so we've lost our edge." He paused. "I agree."

"So I am to fight *carae aeli i'na var* against three *Chi'lan* of your choosing?" she said.

"Yes," Romarin said. "With that, there can be no doubt you are *Chi'lan*. Lochalan will accept the outcome and can't invoke familial right."

Kalena nodded slowly.

Romarin put his good hand on her arm. "Come with me, *chi'li'a*, they will be burning Sillaren's pyre tonight."

Chapter Five

Kalena watched as the flames rose higher into the dark starry night. She had said nothing to Romarin as they walked outside of the gates to the small hillock where the funeral pyres burned.

"*Seh'la Fyrrin*," Romarin Nevfaras said as they crested the small hill. "The fires of death."

Kalena shivered. All around them stood warriors, both ordinary soldiers and *Chi'lan*. She knew that among them were Cahal and Lochalan, but she did not search for them. Standing beside the king made her feel small and inadequate. The pyre was a very real reminder of her mortality.

Kalena knew the hill of *Seh'la Fyrrin*. It was a barren hillside by day, but now it was ringed with torchlight. She had been to too many funerals – almost all *Chi'lan*. The greatest warriors were falling too quickly. She watched as the fire consumed the body, and she closed her eyes. The stench of smoke was overwhelming.

"Do you know why we burn our dead?" Romarin asked her.

"Because Rhyn'athel commands us to," Kalena said, opening her eyes and looking at the king.

"That, but do you know why? Do you know why we don't inter the bodies like those in the north? Or like those who worship Areyn Sehduk?"

Kalena looked back into the flames and then shook her head. "No, I don't."

"It is because Rhyn'athel created us from the flames of the *Fyr*, the fire of creation and destruction. When we die, our spirits become like those flames, only leaving behind this body." He smiled ruefully. "The flames return us to what we really are – creatures created from fire. This is but a transitory world for those of us who serve the warrior god. Unlike Areyn's followers, we do not attach ourselves to this body, for though the spark of life is Rhyn'athel's, our death is Areyn's. We do not keep the body around to remind us of death. There is too much of that in a *Chi'lan's* life."

Kalena looked at Romarin and saw the weariness in his face. *It's the fireworms*, she thought. *He doesn't know how to fight them.* The thought surprised her because Romarin was the son of Rhyn'athel. He, himself, was a godling of incredible power and yet she knew he felt frustrated and angry over what was happening to his people. As she watched the smoke curl upwards, she could empathize with his anger and frustration. How do you slay an unknown enemy?

As she stood shivering in the cold wind, she wondered what kind of *Chi'lan* she would be should she pass the Trials. Romarin would have her fight *Chi'lan*, not *chi'li'a*, and would have her fight to first blood shed. She wondered what Cahal would think of this.

"Kally." Cahal's voice was a little more than a whisper in her ear and she turned to see the King's Champion standing beside her. She glanced at Romarin, who seemed lost in thought and then at Cahal in askance. The *Chi'lan* warrior nodded with his head and she followed him a ways until they were out of earshot.

"Are you all right?" he asked.

"Yes," she said. She glanced at Romarin Nevfaras who seemed to have not noticed she had left. "What of the king?"

"He'll want to be alone tonight," Cahal said knowingly. "Romarin hates it when there is a death – for one death means one less *Chi'lan*."

"I think he feels responsible," she said.

"He does," Cahal admitted. "He thinks there should be some magic that he could use to break Allarun's hold on the beasts, but he can't. No one can, save perhaps Lachlan."

"But Romarin is a son of Rhyn'athel, same as Lachlan," Kalena said.

Cahal nodded. "Yes, but Lachlan was special, Kally. Some say that Romarin is Lachlan's incarnation, but it has yet to be proven."

"You don't think he is."

Cahal smiled grimly. "I'm the only one who doesn't, but then, I am the only one alive who knew Lachlan."

Kalena blinked. "But he has the power of a godling."

"But he has no guidance. Oh, he has learned some magic from the *Laddel* and can control his powers to a certain extent, but he doesn't really know how much power he does have nor does he truly know how to use it."

Kalena stared at the dark form of Romarin, silhouetted against the flames. "I never knew it could be difficult for him to learn how to use his powers." She paused. "Couldn't you teach him?"

Cahal chuckled. "I would if I could. But I am not first-blood, Kally."

"But you knew the warrior god. You taught Lachlan and Elsonre."

"Lachlan was *different*," Cahal said. "Lachlan knew his powers even before they manifested. Even so, he had his mother, Lachlei, to teach him, not that he needed her. You see, he was an incarnation of a much older son of Rhyn'athel. I have seen none of that with Romarin."

"But he has the powers of a godling," she insisted.

"Yes," Cahal said. "He is still trying to learn what they are. He is alone without guidance. I'm surprised I could teach him what I know from memory." He paused. "He needs someone to help him, Kally. Someone who can be an advisor and a friend."

"You're his advisor and friend," Kalena pointed out.

"Yes, but that won't be forever," Cahal said. He smiled at her frown. "Kally, I have no powers to see within the Web of Wyrd, so I do not know my own death. I have lived a very long time, even for an *Eleion*, but I will not live forever. That much Sight, Rhyn'athel has granted me. Romarin will need a champion as strong as me, maybe stronger. You're that champion, Kally."

Kalena stared speechlessly at her mentor. "You can't be serious."

"I am," Cahal said. "Ever since I saw you fight, I knew I had seen it before somewhere. You fight like *Chi'lan* in the old days – someone unafraid of their own death. You are an old soul, Kally, though who you are, I can't fathom. Not Lachlan or Tamar, though your fighting style is like them in ways." He smiled. "Whoever you were, you were *Chi'lan*. As you will be *Chi'lan* again."

Kalena shook her head. "I don't feel old."

"Of course you don't," Cahal said. His face became more serious. "What did Romarin tell you about the Trials?"

"He's changing them. He's having me fight *Chi'lan*."

"*Carae aeli i'na var*," Cahal said quickly. "So, he's decided to put you through the test first."

Kalena nodded.

"You'll do well, but I will have to show you how to fight for this," Cahal said. "We don't want anyone killed."

Chapter Six

Kalena sharpened her sword and stared into the ruddy firelight. She sat on one of the benches in the garrison's great hall not far from the fireplace and watched the flames' reflection play across the flat of her blade. Normally, a *Chi'lan* or even a high-ranking soldier would've taken her bench, but it was springtime and while there was still a chill in the air at night, most of the warriors found no need to sit so close to the fireplace's warmth.

But Kalena was cold. As she ran the whetting stone down the blade, she felt a shiver of anticipation. The Trials were tomorrow and despite all her training and preparation, she was scared. Cahal had tried to teach her the art of cutting without maiming – just enough to draw blood – but it was difficult. Most of the time, her sword hits were too light to wound, just bruise. Cahal had cut her a few times to show her the strength needed for such blows and yet she felt as though she had no control. With the fireworms, she used every bit of her strength – they were the enemy. Here, were her friends.

Her mind kept going back to her conversation with Romarin. Fighting *carae aeli i'na var* against three *Chi'lan* – three of her superiors – scared her. Oh, she had heard Cahal's boast that she could beat any *Chi'lan* – and she had to admit, she was fast enough to best the few *Chi'lan* Cahal had put her up against this year. But was she good enough to best any *Chi'lan*? She thought it not likely. She certainly wasn't better than Cahal. No one was better than Cahal.

There would be a handful of *chi'li'a* going through Trials. The truth was, she did not know who they might be. Cahal had taken her aside and trained her himself, something she knew was special. He seemed more interested in training her with *Chi'lan* than with *chi'li'a*. She knew more *Chi'lan* than apprentices.

Kalena hadn't believed Cahal when he told her Daimhan would throw her out of the infirmary after a few days, and when she found herself after a mere two days back in the garrison, she noticed a different tenor among the soldiers and *chi'li'a*. She wondered if Romarin had made the rule for all *chi'li'a* – not just her.

She had a servant cut her hair for her. Her hair had been singed worse than she originally thought even if she had not planned on cropping her hair as a warrior; she had to do so anyway.

The main doors opened and Kalena looked up to see soldiers salute as a *Chi'lan* entered the garrison. She saw it was Lochalan as he strode into the room and his eyes made contact with hers. He walked towards her and Kalena closed her eyes, wishing she had been in the women's dormitory.

"Kally," Lochalan said. She could see the anger in his eyes and the tightness in his face as he stood over her. She began to rise but he motioned her to stay.

"Brother," she said in greeting.

"How are you feeling?"

She shrugged with a noncommittal grunt and focused all her attention on the blade. It was already sharp, but it gave her something to look at instead of meeting Lochalan's gaze.

Lochalan paused and slipped his hand under her chin. His silver eyes met hers as he raised her chin. Those silver eyes were worried. "Kally," he said. "Be careful tomorrow."

"Are you wishing me luck?"

He smiled. "Of a sort, I suppose," he said. He glanced at the bench. "May I sit beside you?"

"Yes," she said uneasily. She sheathed the blade and looked at Lochalan. *He's going to lecture me again*, she thought ruefully.

Instead, he simply sat and looked at her a long while without speaking. He snorted softly and shook his head. "You know, Kally, it wasn't that long ago when you were my little sister."

"No, it wasn't," she said evenly.

"Sometimes a person fails to see that which is right in front of him."

Kalena said nothing, but gazed at him steadily.

"Look, Kally, I've been thinking about the Trials..." He raised his hand as she started to say something. "Kally, Romarin has upped the stakes – he's having you fight *Chi'lan*..."

"Until first blood shed, yes, I know," Kalena said. "Romarin told me himself."

"And you *agreed* to this?" Lochalan could barely contain his rage. "Kally, do you know who he'll put you up against?"

"It doesn't matter," Kalena said. "I'm good enough."

"Yes, you're good enough to be *Chi'lan*, but gods, Kally, no one has done this since Nevfaras' decree."

"Romarin has," Kalena said. "Actually, not as *Chi'lan* but as king. He was challenged, didn't you know that?"

"Yes, but that is Romarin."

"Cahal says I'm a better fighter than Romarin."

"Cahal is a fool."

Without thinking, Kalena's fist shot out and her knuckles impacted Lochalan's jaw. The impact threw Lochalan off the bench and he sat on the floor staring up at her half-dazed.

Kalena had drawn her sword and pointed the tip at her brother's face. "How *dare* you insult Cahal!"

The hall grew very quiet. She heard the rasps of swords drawn but did not turn to look. "Don't be a fool, Kally," Lochalan said softly. "Put the sword away."

Kalena lowered her sword and felt strong arms grab her and disarm her. Soldiers and warriors swarmed around them, splitting the two up. Once or twice, she heard Lochalan call her name as they shackled her hands. She did not resist as they led her away.

Chapter Seven

Kalena sat in the small cell in the dungeon of Citadel Heights and pondered her fate. She had made a terrible mistake, she decided. Assaulting a *Chi'lan*, even if it was her brother, was a serious offense for a *chi'li'a*. An offense that would end her career as a *Chi'lan* and probably as a soldier. No one could blame Romarin for expelling her from the *Chi'lan*, or even exiling her now.

She cursed the warrior god for doing this to her. How could Rhyn'athel have let her lose her temper so? Kalena had trained to be a *Chi'lan* for so many years and was now looking at having a single action end her career. She closed her eyes, trying not to let the tears well up. *I am a soldier*, she thought. *I should not cry*.

Patience, a voice inside her said. *Patience is key*. She knew that Lochalan had come to apologize to her. She knew he had come to offer an apology and to point out the dangers, and instead she punched him for insulting Cahal. *He deserved it too*, she thought smugly. Lochalan had no business insulting the King's Champion.

There was nothing to do but sit and wait. The cell was cold and damp – not much bigger than a six by six hole really, but she had found a small patch by the far wall which wasn't too wet . There was not much light – just a little from the barred ten-inch square window in the door. She could still see and spent her time counting the blocks in the wall. She was somewhere in the hundreds when she finally fell into an uneasy sleep.

"I know she attacked a *Chi'lan*," Cahal said. "But it was Lochalan and no doubt he provoked her."

Romarin looked sidelong at his champion and shook his head. "I can't have my warriors attacking each other, Cahal."

They were standing on the wall walk, watching the sunrise over the plains in the east. Romarin ignored the salutes of soldiers and *Chi'lan* as he passed.

"Tamar attacked Rhyn'athel once," Cahal said, walking beside him.

"When Rhyn'athel was in mortal guise, Tamar attacked him with a dagger."

"I know the story," Romarin said. "But Lachlei was queen then and had many more *Chi'lan* than I do—and she didn't actually see the fight."

"But everyone knew about it and all the *Chi'lan* saw," Cahal said. "I was there. I know. Rhyn'athel bested Tamar and everyone agreed Rhyn'athel was one of us after that."

"The old ways were not necessarily better," Romarin said. He turned to see Lochalan approaching them both. "I suppose you want me to grant leniency to your sister."

Lochalan frowned. "Kally's a bit of a hothead. She deserves to rot in that dungeon a while, but I'll admit I provoked her..."

"I don't want a *Chi'lan* who would attack another," Romarin said. "She can't go through Trials."

"It was a mistake," Cahal said. "We all make mistakes at that age. Surely you can appreciate that." His gaze fell on Romarin's silver hand.

Romarin clenched his fist, feeling his face flush. "If you were anyone other than whom you were..."

"You'd kill me?" said Cahal wryly. "Come now, Romarin, she made a mistake. Delay the Trial if necessary – a year, two years – whatever, but don't deny a born *Chi'lan* the opportunity."

Romarin turned to Lochalan. "What do you say? You've invoked familial right with her; now you have responsibility over her. What should I do?"

Lochalan frowned. Romarin could see he had not expected this question. "Kalena is my sister. Even though she is a bit temperamental, I deserved the blow."

Romarin arched an eyebrow. "Really? What did you say?"

Lochalan was about to answer when a cry rang out from the watchtowers. "Fireworms!"

"Oh, by Rhyn'athel's mane!" Romarin swore. He turned to Cahal, but his champion was already barking out orders to the soldiers along the wall walk. Romarin drew his sword and looked up in time to see a dark form heading right towards him. He barely had time to raise the blade before the fireworm smashed into him, tearing through cloak and raking its venom talons across his armor.

Romarin slammed his adamantine blade into the creature, severing its leg. The fireworm screamed and snapped at him, trying to throw its coils around his body. But Romarin was quick and slashed at the coils. His sword hacked though the spine and the creature collapsed, half-paralyzed and floundering on the ground. Romarin grasped the fireworm's neck with his gauntleted hand and thrust the blade up through its snapping jaw and into the skull. Dark blood spurted from the wound as the creature tried to shake its head from Romarin's grasp. The gauntlet held tight and the light dimmed from the worm's eyes.

Romarin stepped from the fray and turned to see how others fared. Through the fight, he knew there had been other fireworms – now he saw the full extent of the attack. There were at least five fireworms other than the one he fought. Cahal was standing over a downed *Chi'lan* warrior not far from him, protecting the man from another attacking fireworm. Other warriors and soldiers were fighting desperately.

Romarin charged forward, swing his sword as the fireworm lunged at Cahal. His sword bit into the creature's neck, but it had sensed him and turned at the last moment. Flames issued from the creature's mouth barely missing Romarin and setting his cloak on fire. But the sword had done its damage, cutting into the trachea and effectively quenching the flames.

Romarin tore his cloak off and tossed it aside. The creature screamed and attacked Romarin but Cahal leapt at it, slamming *Fyren* into the fireworm's spine and severing the spinal cord. The creature floundered and fell. Cahal ignored it, kneeling beside the fallen warrior. He turned the *Chi'lan* over. The man's face was burned beyond recognition.

"Romarin, help him!" Cahal shouted to Romarin.

Romarin shuddered as he looked at the *Chi'lan* and shook his head. "He's gone, Cahal."

"No he's not, damn you!" Cahal shouted. "Heal him!"

Romarin stared at Cahal in incredulity. He looked back at the man and realization dawned on him. The man wore captain insignia.

"It's Lochalan," Cahal said. "You've got to save him."

Chapter Eight

The infirmary was filled with wounded now. Daimhan and the other healers did their best to heal warriors but it was Romarin who seemed to be needed most. He went from wounded *Chi'lan* to wounded soldier, trying to heal them the best he could so the healers could take over. When he lacked strength, he called on others to grasp his sword and using it as a conduit to use their strength to heal the wounded.

"What of Lochalan?" Cahal said as Romarin stood up from another wounded *Chi'lan*.

"Is he still alive?" Romarin asked, dreading the answer.

"Yes, but just barely," Cahal said. "You must do something."

Romarin nodded. "I'll need your help."

Cahal met his gaze steadily. "I know. I'm ready." He held out his sword in offering.

Romarin walked slowly over to the blackened lump of flesh that was Lochalan and sat down. "I would normally not do this."

"Do it!" Cahal snapped. "He can't die. Not now."

Romarin gripped the blade with his right hand and pressed his good hand against Lochalan's flesh. Lochalan screamed in pain and tried to thrash, but the healers had already bound him to the cot.

:*Easy*, Romarin said in mindspeak. :*You have the will to live.*

:*Romarin?* Lochalan's mental voice was weak but still there. :*What have I become?*

:*Hang on, Chi'lan*, Romarin said. He felt the familiar warming glow of his powers as he ran his hand across the man's charred skin. He too felt the strength flow from Cahal as he did. Lochalan had an extraordinary will to live for one not born of first-blood lines and Romarin marveled at the man's strength. Lochalan's skin began to regrow beneath Romarin's hand. The damage had been primarily burns, but they would have been sufficient enough to kill most *Eleion*. But Lochalan wanted to live, and Romarin had to admire that inner strength as well.

When at last Romarin felt Lochalan was no longer in danger, he pulled away and felt his energy leave him. He slumped in the chair and looked over at Cahal, who looked exhausted as well. Cahal was very old for an *Eleion* but was also very strong in spirit. Some *Eleion* aged poorly but *Chi'lan* warriors like Cahal seemed to grow more powerful as they grew older. Perhaps it was the warrior god, himself, that kept the *Chi'lan* so powerful. Cahal *had* been a close friend to the god.

"I don't know how you do it," Cahal muttered. His face was pale from the exertion.

"Nor do I," Romarin said. "Yet somehow we find a way."

Cahal smiled and took a tonic that one of the healers gave him and drank it. When the healer tried to press a cup into Romarin's hands, the king waved him off. "Drink, Romarin," Cahal ordered him. "You won't gain your strength back by neglecting yourself."

Romarin reluctantly took the cup, took a swig and spat it out. Cahal laughed. He glared at the older man. "I won't gain my strength back drinking this swill either," he said. He eyed the cup suspiciously. "What's in it?"

"Herbs..."

"Poisonroot, no doubt," Romarin muttered.

"Old wine."

"They can't use good wine? It tastes like vinegar."

"Probably is," Cahal said. "They know better than to give a first-blood alcohol."

"Right." Romarin set the cup down on the floor and using the chair as a brace hauled himself to his feet. He staggered and Cahal caught him before he fell. "Damn!" Romarin snapped. "I can stand."

Cahal nodded and let go, letting the king test his legs while holding the chair. "Maybe I shouldn't have insisted." He glanced back at Lochalan. Daimhan was wrapping the wounded *Chi'lan*'s face carefully with clean bandages.

"No, you should've," Romarin said. "We've lost five *Chi'lan* in this attack."

"Five?" Cahal's face showed the horror. "Five? But we only have..."

Romarin nodded. "I've healed soldiers too, Cahal. We lost more than thirty soldiers." He paused. "We have to do something, Cahal. These damn lizards are destroying our warriors."

Cahal looked back at Lochalan. "Will he live?"

"He should," Romarin said. "But he won't be available for duty for weeks until he regains his strength." He paused. "There are ten *Chi'lan* wounded here."

"Out of the twenty-seven left? We're short more than half our number," Cahal said. He looked at the king.

"Our numbers have always been small since Lachlan's defeat on Darkling Plain," Romarin said.

"But never below fifty until Allarun slew Nevfaras. My friend, you must try again. You're a son of Rhyn'athel..." Cahal was cut off by Romarin's withering look.

"No, it is not Allarun who sends this plague on us," Romarin said, his voice quiet and steady, belying the anger and frustration he felt. "The Sight has told me that much."

"Then, what?"

Romarin shook his head and turned away. "I don't have the ability to read the Web of Wyrd like my sire – or like Lachlan," he added bitterly.

"Maybe you should stop trying to live up to them," Cahal said.

Romarin looked at Cahal. "What do you mean?"

"You are Romarin Nevfaras, son of the warrior god. Stop trying so hard to be Lachlan and be Romarin Nevfaras," Cahal said softly so only Romarin heard. "Finding your own path to your powers is far more important than trying to achieve another's greatness."

A silence followed and Romarin lowered his head. When he looked up, he met Cahal's gaze. He nodded slowly and glanced at Lochalan. "You're right, as always, old friend."

"What do you know about the worms?" Cahal asked.

"They are somehow tied to Nevfaras' death. But how, I can't say," Romarin shrugged.

"But they do not come from Allarun?"

"No, not directly, though I suspect Allarun doesn't mind if the fireworms attack us."

"I could lead some *Chi'lan* to find the source of the attacks." He sat back in the chair.

Romarin shook his head. "No, of all the *Chi'lan*, you are indispensable. And even if I did allow it – what warriors would we use? We have only a dozen left who are healthy."

"Kalena is ready for trials. A number of other *chi'li'a* could go through Trials within a year if I were to accelerate their training..." Cahal began.

"Kalena is in my dungeon," Romarin reminded him. "And I am not sure we have a year left."

"Then the choice is yours to act or not," Cahal said. They both stood up and walked slowly out of the infirmary. "We already know what inaction will do."

Chapter Nine

Kalena awoke to the sound of keys and the cell door opening. She blinked as the bright, smoky torchlight filled her little room. A *Shara'kai* guard peered in. She was a great deal shorter and stockier than Kalena and had pale gold hair and light blue eyes. "*Chi'li'a* Kalena?"

Kalena scrambled to her feet, but found her back and legs sore. She rubbed them as she stood up. "Yes?"

"Champion Cahal wants to see you."

Kalena would have flung her arms around the woman's neck and kissed her for joy had she not been so cold and stiff. "He wants to see me?"

The woman nodded. "I thought they were daft throwing a warrior here – what'd you do?"

"Punched my brother," Kalena said.

The *Shara'kai* laughed and then quickly became sober. Her pale eyes glittered in the torchlight with concern. "Your brother's Captain Lochalan, isn't he?"

"Yes, why?" Kalena said, a sinking feeling settled in her stomach. She could not read minds, but she knew how to read expressions and posture. Something had gone terribly wrong.

"I think you need to ask Cahal," the guard said. "Follow me." She turned and beckoned her out of the cell. Kalena followed.

"There's been a fireworm attack," Kalena stated. It was more of a hunch than anything, but she knew it was unlikely her brother would be injured or killed any other way. "Is Lochalan all right?"

The guard shook her head. "I don't know – there were rumors that a number of *Chi'lan* and soldiers got killed. I've heard a lot of warriors were injured too."

Kalena chewed her lip. *They're rumors*, she reminded herself. *Just rumors.* She glanced at the guard and noticed there were no rank insignia. The woman was a common foot soldier. It was unlikely that she would have news, but she could have heard something indirectly, even working in the dungeons.

As Kalena followed the woman to the garrison, she began to wonder why she was freed. Would Cahal have brought her out of the dungeon simply to be told her brother was dead and put right back in? Or maybe she would be told her sentence. Her mind whirled with fear.

The guard brought Kalena to a small room normally reserved for captains' offices in the garrison. The guard knocked and opened the door. Cahal was standing in the room. There were a few benches and a fireplace, but nothing else. Cahal looked serious.

"Thank you, Mira, you may leave."

The guard bowed once and left, shutting the door.

Kalena stood uneasily before Cahal as he stared at her with his steady silver eyes. There was a cut along his face that had recently been sewn up: there had been a fireworm attack. She took a breath in and let it out slowly as he stared at her. Even so, her breath sounded like a ragged gasp.

"You know what you did was wrong," Cahal said without preamble.

"Yes, Champion," she whispered.

"What?"

"Yes, Champion," she said louder. Her voice cracked.

Cahal approached her, frowning as he did so. "You know that Romarin Nevfaras was willing to let you rot in that cell for that outburst of yours."

"Yes, Champion."

"I couldn't talk him out of it either. Unfortunately for us – and oddly fortunately for you – fireworms attacked."

Kalena held her breath. The blood was pounding in her ears.

"What have I told you about holding your breath?" Cahal chided her.

"You told me it's the quickest way to drop me to the ground, along with locking my knees."

"Then, breathe."

"Permission to speak?" Kalena asked. She breathed in slowly and tried to exhale. To her ears, it sounded noisy.

"No," Cahal said. "I'm not finished. We lost five *Chi'lan* this morning." He paused and saw her reaction. "No, Lochalan wasn't killed but he was severely injured along with nine other *Chi'lan*. It has put us at a serious disadvantage."

Severely injured? Kalena felt sick. *Breathe. Breathe.*

"He's alive but he's in no shape to fight at this time," Cahal said.

"Romarin agrees that we need warriors. That means you'll be going through the Trials tomorrow – if you're up to it."

Kalena's heart beat faster. The terrible deaths meant they had no choice but to make *chi'li'a* into *Chi'lan*. That is, if they passed the Trials. "I'm up to it, Champion."

"Good," Cahal said. "Go get cleaned up. You stink of dungeon. You can see Lochalan afterwards. Then after dinner, we'll see how well you fight."

It was later afternoon when Kalena made her way to the infirmary. She had taken a hot bath – something she needed after a night in the dungeon. Her body had ached where she had contact with the stone and the hot water had provided some relief. Now she walked up the stairwell and into the infirmary.

Cahal had already warned her that Lochalan had been burned badly, but she had not expected what she saw. The healers left the bandages off his charred skin where the new skin was now growing. A black burnt layer lay on her brother's newly formed skin like a snake's molting. It was sloughing. Kalena turned away. The stench of charred flesh and hair was overwhelming.

"It's pretty bad," said Daimhan's voice beside her.

Kalena looked at the *Shara'kai* and shuddered. "He's worse than Sillaren was."

"Romarin says he had a stronger will to live," Daimhan replied. "It looks worse than it is. Romarin managed to regenerate the skin beneath the old one so he'll look better once the old skin is off."

"Why don't you take it off now?" she asked.

The healer shook his head. "The new skin is too fragile. It'll take days for it to fully heal. In the meantime, the old skin provides a protective layer. That and our salves."

She looked back at it in morbid curiosity. "Does it hurt?"

"A bit. But it'll itch more. The main problem is the loss of water in his body. We can barely get him awake to drink water or broth."

Kalena nodded. "Do you want me to try?"

Daimhan shook his head. "Most of the fluids we give him have heavy sedatives to keep him from feeling the pain. I doubt he'll be conscious."

"Well, I'd still like to sit beside him."

Daimhan nodded. "Go ahead."

Kalena walked over and sat beside Lochalan. She was surprised to see his eyes open. They were bloodshot and glazed over from the medication. "Kal..."

"Shhh!" Kalena said. "I'm here. Romarin freed me after the attack."

"I'm dy-dying?"

"No, you're not. Cahal says Romarin saved you."

Lochalan closed his eyes. Kalena resisted the urge to touch him. She knew it would cause him pain and might actually cause an infection. "Pyre," he rasped.

"What?"

"No burial. Pyre."

"You're not dying."

"Promise me." He opened his silver eyes again and met hers earnestly. "Promise."

Kalena shook her head. "You're not dying, but I promise anyway. No burials."

He closed his eyes again and fell asleep. She could see his mouth turn slightly upwards in a smile.

She sat there for some time just watching him breathe. She knew he would not die now but she also wondered how long it would be before he was sufficiently healed. He would bear some ugly scars for it, that she knew.

Kalena stood up and stretched. It was time for dinner and to seek Cahal out to prepare for the morning trials.

Chapter Ten

The next morning Kalena stood in full mail facing the rising sun. Sowelu dawned blood red as if in anticipation of the Trials to come. All around her stood the *Chi'lan* warriors – a pitiful few – not even two dozen – where a few centuries before, the *Chi'lan* had been hundreds strong. In Lachlan's time, the *Chi'lan* had numbered in the thousands.

Cahal and Romarin had chosen the hill of *Seh'la Fyrrin* for the *Chi'lan* Trials outside the walls of Citadel Heights. Cahal had told her it reminded him of the hill not far from the ruins of Caer Lachlanel, the ancestral home of the *Lochvaur* that was razed not long after Lachlan's death. Where that hill had been forested, the hill of *Seh'la Fyrrin* was barren. The pyres had blackened the dirt and although Kalena neither had the power nor the Sight of a first-blood, she could feel the death around her. She smiled as she recalled Cahal's statement that he believed her to be a reincarnation of another *Chi'lan* warrior. She only half-believed it; it was more comforting to think she was just Kalena and nothing more. She certainly did not come from a special bloodline like Romarin did.

She looked at each warrior. As she looked from face to face at each *Chi'lan*, she realized how tired they looked. The fireworms had beaten each of them into a fatalistic submission – the same sentiment she felt when she had talked to her brother. There were four women and eight men, not counting Romarin or Cahal. They ringed her as she stood on the opposite side of Romarin and Cahal. Kalena was armed only with a broadsword and a dagger.

She had gotten no sleep that night after training with Cahal. She had been too keyed up to rest, wondering who Romarin would have her fight. Cahal had gone over rudimentary sword fighting and had her practice the various sword katas she had learned since becoming apprenticed as a *chi'li'a*. Kalena knew these katas by rote as well as how to fight in any situation. But the trials were different. This was a test of *Chi'lan* against *chi'li'a*.

Breakfast had been nothing more than hot tea and a small piece of bread. Her stomach had rebelled against anything more substantial. As she stood ready for the fight, she tried to remember Cahal's advice from the previous night.

"No matter who you're up against, remember that they're an opponent," Cahal said. *"Until you fight them, even the most unassuming farmer with a knife can be dangerous until you have a chance to assess their skill. At the same time, even those with renowned skills have weaknesses. Lachlan, for example, wouldn't feint enough to draw you in. He relied solely on his ability to intimidate by pressing forward. He could do it and risk injury. You can't."*

Kalena nodded to herself. Lachlan was the greatest *Eleion* warrior and yet he had been taken by surprise.

Romarin strode forward. To her surprise, he was in full armor like the other *Chi'lan*. Instead of a crown, he wore an open-faced helm. "The Trials have always been a sacred initiation into becoming *Chi'lan*. Since Lochvaur drew his blade across his arm and swore a blood oath to Rhyn'athel on proving his loyalty, so the *Chi'lan* have made the blood oath to the god. It is an oath we do not take lightly nor can it be rescinded. Once you become *Chi'lan*, you are bound to the oath for eternity. It is not an oath that can be broken without repercussions. The warrior god is patient and will choose the time for such reckoning. Are you willing to step into the ring and take such an oath?"

"I am," Kalena said.

"Good," Romarin said. "You will fight three *Chi'lan* of my choosing. The fight will be *carae aeli i'na var* – until first blood shed. The challenge is not necessarily to defeat your opponents – most *chi'li'a* cannot stand up to battle-hardened *Chi'lan*, but to show skill. In order to become *Chi'lan* you must demonstrate you can fight like a *Chi'lan*. Do you understand?"

"I do." She shifted from one foot to the other nervously. At least she did not have to defeat a *Chi'lan*.

"Good," said Romarin. "You will fight each opponent. Once first blood is drawn, even if a scratch, we will stop the fight and attend to the wound, if required. Then if you are ready, we will continue. If there is a life-threatening or fatal blow by either warrior, the fight will stop. If you inflict such a wound, you will not become *Chi'lan*. A *Chi'lan* who deals such a blow will have his or her fate decided by a vote from the other *Chi'lan*. So it has been since Lochvaur's time, so it is now. Do you understand?"

Kalena shivered. "I do."

"Good, get ready, *chi'li'a*. Your first opponent is Captain Elsayr." With that, a woman *Shara'kai Chi'lan* who had green eyes and olive-colored skin stepped forward. Kalena nearly gasped – of all the women Elsayr was the strongest and the best Captain behind perhaps Lochalan.

Elsayer was as strong as a pureblood *Eleion* man. Kalena remembered Lochalan tell her about the *Shara'kai* when he first met her. Any reservations about Elsayr being half-blood quickly disappeared when Lochalan saw her fight. The woman's mail was tarnished and looked as though it had been repaired several times – a testament to her many fights with fireworms. Her helm was dented in one place and covered her short-cropped hair. She drew her sword and stood opposite of Kalena. Kalena drew her broadsword, feeling less confident. They bowed to each other.

Romarin withdrew and awaited their nods. Elsayr nodded once and fixed her gaze on Kalena. Kalena nodded also.

"Begin!" Romarin said.

Elsayr sprung into action, starting forward towards Kalena. Kalena moved aside, not willing to meet the *Shara'kai* on her own terms just yet. Elsayr pressed the attack and Kalena sidled away, hoping to get some feel for the woman's skill. The woman pressed again and Kalena dodged the swift thrust and countered with a slash. Elsayr parried and attacked and Kalena found herself driven backwards.

The sword felt heavy in her hands and her mouth was dry. Kalena was sure that Cahal was shaking his head seeing his best student so intimidated. Elsayr slammed her sword towards Kalena's knee. Kalena stepped aside, swinging her own blade. To her surprise, the blade raked across Elsayr's chest and the *Chi'lan* yelped and jumped back.

Kalena blinked in surprise and leapt forward, swinging her own sword. The rake had not been enough to draw blood, but it was enough to show Elsayr had left a hole for Kalena to take advantage of now. Kalena used the momentum to press her attack, this time gaining in confidence with each sword thrust.

Kalena could see that Elsayr realized her folly and tried to recover the attack again, but Kalena was not going to allow the woman to gain advantage of the situation. At one point, Elsayr feinted and Kalena held back. Then Elsayr moved in for an attack. Kalena leapt forward and swung her blade and Elsayr tried again at Kalena's knee. This time, Kalena's sword slammed into Elsayr's gauntleted hand. The force caused the *Chi'lan* to yelp and drop her sword.

"Halt!" said Romarin.

Elsayr's hand was limp and she was shaking. She pulled her hand from the gauntlet. It was apparent that the force of Kalena's sword had broken the bones in her hand. A thin weal of blood trickled from where the sword had sliced into the gauntlet.

"*I'na var,*" said Romarin.

Elsayr bowed to Kalena and moved from the circle. She went to Romarin who touched her hand for a brief instant before taking her place next to the other *Chi'lan*. Kalena waited, wondering who would be the next *Chi'lan* to enter. Her heart hammered in her ears when she saw Cahal enter on the opposite side and bow to her.

Chapter Eleven

Kalena bowed back, feeling numb. She knew there was no way she could defeat her teacher. Surely, Cahal knew this. Cahal knew all her strengths and weaknesses and would take advantage of them.

If Cahal were a lesser man, he might have gone easy on her to make his skill as a teacher look good. But Kalena knew Cahal better than that and knew he would give her a nasty scar across her face if he thought she was not performing up to his standards.

Her teacher was steely-eyed and his expression a mask as he met her gaze. Kalena forced herself to look into those dark gray eyes and forced herself to regard him as an opponent. She tried to remember Cahal's story of Lachlan's *Chi'lan* Trial. At age fifteen, Lachlan had drawn first blood on Cahal when Cahal was the teacher. Cahal had shown her the scar on his arm from those Trials so long ago.

Cahal drew his sword, *Fyren*, and stood ready. The old sword with its stained adamantine blade seemed to glow with power as Cahal held it. It was not a magical blade, per se, but it was one that had killed demons and had even wounded the death god.

"Ready?" Romarin asked. Cahal nodded once. Kalena did not dare let her gaze wander as she nodded. Cahal was stronger than her by far, but he was slower. She had used that to her advantage in sparring against him with some success. The trick was to get the cut in before his skill as a warrior drove her into a calculated position of weakness. She felt her body coil; the only way she would win is if she used her speed against the older *Chi'lan*.

"Begin!" Romarin said and Kalena shot forward like an arrow leaving the string. She flew at Cahal, swinging her sword and causing her mentor to retreat backwards, parrying her blows. Cahal stepped to the side and Kalena followed, forcing him into a greater retreat. But as she did, she recognized the subtle shift in Cahal's stance – he let her pour out her energy, watching when to make the shift from defense to attack.

Cahal dropped his sword ever so slightly as though he might attack, leaving a small but crucial opening. Kalena lunged, hoping to slip the sword by him when he closed the gap. It was too late when Kalena realized that this was a feint and she had fallen for it. Cahal's sword drove into her hand as she forced the sword forward. The blade sliced into the leather and she yelped as the tip cut deep.

"*I'na var!*" said Romarin.

They lowered their weapons and Kalena stuck her sword in the ground and held her bleeding hand. She could tell it was bruised badly and possibly one or more bones were broken. Bright red blood flowed from the gauntlet – Cahal had hit an artery. She applied pressure, hoping to stem the bleeding.

"Come here, both of you," Romarin said.

Kalena glanced at Cahal and for the first time realized, he too was holding his hand. He was grinning despite the obvious pain. Kalena walked up to the king expecting an admonishment. Instead, he turned to her. "Hold out your hand."

She was cradling her right hand like a wounded sparrow but she obliged. Romarin placed his left hand on top of hers and she saw his hand glowed with power. All at once, the pain was gone and she could move her fingers again.

Next Cahal held his hand up for Romarin to see. The gauntlet was shredded and blood oozed from it. Romarin chuckled as he touched his friend's hand and healed it.

"Are you sure you wish to be embarrassed?" Cahal said. "She's quick."

"And you're getting old," Romarin chided him. "Get your sword." Cahal nodded and retrieved *Fyren*. Kalena went to her ready position and waited. What she saw stunned her even more than Cahal fighting her. Cahal took Romarin's place and Romarin Nevfaras took the place opposite of her and drew his sword. Romarin bowed to her.

A shocked murmur ran through the *Chi'lan*. Kalena froze. She was expected to *fight* the king? She glanced at Cahal who gave her no indication what to do next. She bowed stiffly and waited.

"Ready?" Cahal asked.

Romarin nodded. Cahal turned to Kalena, who nodded, feeling numb inside. Could she possibly out-fight the king, himself? He was the son of the warrior god. How did he fight? What if she actually drew blood? She nodded once. How was she to plan her attack?

"Begin!" Cahal said.

Romarin swung his sword twice as he started towards her; the arcing sword flashed in the morning sun. His silver gauntlet gleamed with an unearthly power. Romarin walked forward: confident and unyielding. Kalena circled, eyeing Romarin warily. She knew he had to be a good fighter – Cahal only trained the best and only the greatest *Chi'lan* would be king. And Romarin was the son of Rhyn'athel, the warrior god. His skill would have to surpass any mortal.

Then Romarin leapt forward, swinging the two-handed blade with his left hand. Kalena nearly gasped as she watched him move – she had never seen a warrior so strong as to wield a bastard sword one-handed. She dodged the blade as it arced towards her and swung her own broadsword. Romarin caught it with his right hand and ripped the blade from her hands as he did so. The silver gauntlet did not show a scratch or nick as he tossed her sword aside. Kalena drew her dagger and backed away. It was woefully inadequate against a warrior like Romarin. He charged at her, swinging the two-handed blade.

Never in her life had Kalena been more terrified. She saw the sword flash and dodged, barely missing the blade as it followed her movement. She rolled once and landed on her feet. Romarin lunged after her. She spun on her heels and led him in a chase towards her own blade that lay on the ground just out of reach.

Before she could scramble to her sword, he caught her and the blade came down. At that moment, Kalena threw her dagger. It was a hard throw and the dagger was not made for throwing but it tumbled and caught Romarin's shoulder, its blade just pricking through the mail and into the arming shirt beneath. The batting protected him against the cut. She was disarmed and had nowhere to go.

Romarin held her at swordpoint. "Yield."

"Halt," said Cahal. He turned to the king. "This was not a fair fight."

Romarin raised an eyebrow. "It wasn't?"

"No. No other *Chi'lan* could've disarmed her the way you did."

Romarin grinned. He looked at Kalena. "What do you think, *chi'li'a*?"

Kalena swallowed hard and glanced from Cahal to Romarin. "Real life isn't fair," she said at last. "There will be opponents a *Chi'lan* faces who will not fight fairly." She looked at Cahal. "King Romarin defeated me according to the terms of the Trials. I will not contest."

Romarin plunged the two-handed sword into the ground. He offered her his left hand. "Arise, *Chi'lan* Kalena. And may the gods help anyone who picks a fight with you."

Chapter Twelve

Kalena's head spun as she took Romarin's proffered hand and allowed him to hoist her to her feet. *Chi'lan?* She looked at Cahal who grinned and nodded. Romarin walked over to her sword and picked it up. He strode over to her, holding it flat between his two hands. He held the sword out to her as though offering it.

Kalena stepped forward and reached out to touch the blade. As her hands grasped the sword, she felt it hum with power. But how could it? It was an ordinary blade, albeit forged from fine adamantine. As she stared into Romarin's eyes, she felt the world fall away and she was no longer standing on the hill of *Seh'la Fyrrin* in the bright sunshine, but beneath the stars on top of a windswept mountain. She was standing beneath a large, gnarled tree with silver bark and branches that stretched across the sky. From the branches spun threads, thin as gossamer that wove into the very fabric of the world. Kalena almost leapt back but caught herself as a strong voice rang in her ears.

:*Do not release the blade, Chi'lan.*

Kalena looked up at Romarin – but the man who stood before her was not the king. He was larger than even Romarin Nevfaras and while there was a strong resemblance between the two, Kalena could feel the power behind this warrior. He was handsome and muscularly built with a flowing red-gold mane and silver eyes. The sword she was touching was not her own, but a Sword of Power. The runes glowed along the edge of the blade, spelling its name: *Teiwaz*.

Kalena was speechless. The man she had taken to be Romarin at first was not. It was the warrior god, Rhyn'athel.

The god smiled at her; it was not an unkind smile and despite her terror, Kalena met his gaze. "This is not the first time you've taken this vow to me," he said.

Kalena blinked. Memories of another life flooded her mind as she met the god's gaze. Everything of her former life came back to her, both bad and good. She wanted to shout and to weep at the same time. To be angry at the god for what she had gone through and her thankfulness at being given another chance at life. Her mouth became dry and she found it difficult to speak. "No, it is not."

He nodded. "There are those who do not wish you to become *Chi'lan*. Your brother, for one."

The memories of Kalena's former life tried to mix and mingle with her own. Kalena struggled with them, trying to keep the two separated but to little avail. "But he is not my brother."

"Not in your former life but this one." His tone was gentle, almost chiding.

Kalena nodded.

"You have as much right as anyone to refuse this vow, if you wish. I will not hold you to it," Rhyn'athel said. "Now that you remember who you were and what happened, it is up to you to decide if you still wish to be *Chi'lan*. Elisila has a claim to you as much as I do, but it is your choice, Kalena. No one else's."

Kalena lowered her eyes to the glowing sword. "If I have returned, then surely it means that Lachlan has. Is he Romarin?"

"What do you think?" Rhyn'athel asked.

Kalena shook her head. "I don't know."

"Romarin is my son; that much I will say. But his way is uncertain and he needs someone strong to stand with him in battle. That person is you, Kalena. Until Lachlan returns."

She nodded. "Very well, Rhyn'athel. Until Lachlan returns."

He smiled. "And tell Cahal I have not forgotten his friendship. He has been like a brother to me." He paused. "Repeat the vow."

The words echoed in her head. "I am *Chi'lan* Kalena, daughter of *Chi'lan*, sister of *Chi'lan*. My life, my soul, my sword belongs to Rhyn'athel for eternity. I swear to live as Rhyn'athel directs me. I pledge loyalty to my fellow *Chi'lan* and to my king, never to betray them..."

The fire from the Sword, *Teiwaz*, glowed bright blue and enveloped her. She passed out; feeling knees buckle and she collapse on the hill of *Seh'la Fyrrin*.

Romarin stared in disbelief as the moment Kalena touched the sword, her eyes glazed and she fell into a trance. He was about to speak the words of the vow for her to repeat and yet, she was talking to someone

– not him – and she spoke in the *Athel'cen* tongue – the language of the gods.

"No, it is not," she said, speaking in *Athel'cen*.

Cahal walked up to her. "Kally?"

Kalena stared glassy-eyed ahead. "But he is not my brother."

Romarin drew his hands back to move the blade from beneath her hands but Cahal gripped his arm. "Don't – I've seen this before."

"How does she know *Athel'cen*?" Romarin asked.

"If I have returned, then surely it means that Lachlan has. Is he Romarin?" Kalena asked, unseeing.

Romarin shot a look at Cahal, whose face was grim. "Who is she talking to?"

"Rhyn'athel," said Cahal softly. A murmur ran through the *Chi'lan*. Cahal raised his hand for silence.

Kalena shook her head imperceptibly. "I don't know."

Romarin stared at the woman before him – he would have referred to her as a girl if he had not seen her fight. She was speaking with his father: something he had failed to do most of his life. And now she was asking the god if Romarin was the foretold champion of the Prophecy. He swallowed hard. What would she tell him when this was done?

She nodded. "Very well, Rhyn'athel. Until Lachlan returns."

Again, Romarin met Cahal's gaze. Cahal's face was unreadable.

Then, Kalena began to recite the *Chi'lan* vow. "I am *Chi'lan* Kalena, daughter of *Chi'lan*, sister of *Chi'lan*. My life, my soul, my sword belongs to Rhyn'athel for eternity. I swear to live as Rhyn'athel directs me. I pledge loyalty to my fellow *Chi'lan* and to my king, never to betray them..."

The sword Romarin was holding pulsed fiery blue and then white-hot. It burned his hand and he dropped the sword with a cry. Kalena's eyes rolled back and she collapsed onto the ground.

Chapter Thirteen

"I thought you said she knew nothing of the *Athel'cen* language," Kalena heard Romarin's voice somewhere through the haze.

"She doesn't," Cahal's voice came to her mind.

"You didn't teach her the *Chi'lan* vow?"

"Of course not." Cahal said, his voice obviously affronted. "Why would I do that?"

Silence ensued. "She mentioned my name and Lachlan's in the same breath."

"There have been a handful of *Chi'lan* who have fallen under such trances and spoke directly with the warrior god. Most remember little of their conversations. Either the strain was too great or the god removes their memory."

"Could this be a hoax?" Romarin asked.

"How? Kalena has no magic – you've sensed this yourself. You can hear her thoughts."

Romarin sighed. "You're right. She has none which makes the flames even more puzzling."

"How's your hand?"

"Fine. See? Not a burn mark."

Kalena groaned. Her head was beginning to pound as the haze cleared. What had exactly happened? She remembered standing there under the night sky with the huge tree looming over both her and the god as it spun a web that coursed through the world. She remembered Rhyn'athel had said she had served him once before.

She tried to remember the memories that he had given her. She was a *Chi'lan* – she could remember a battle she fought beside two brothers who wielded Swords of Power. One was Romarin...

"Kally?" Cahal asked.

Her eyes fluttered open to bright light and she winced and shut them tight, groaning again. She recognized the infirmary. "Cahal?" Her voice was raspy.

"Yes, Kally, I'm here," Cahal said.

She opened her eyes and looked into the old warrior's face. Romarin was sitting not far from her, his eyes narrowed. *How much did they hear?*

"We heard your side," Romarin said, not bothering to hide his annoyance or the fact he had plucked her unguarded thoughts from her mind.

"But you did not hear Rhyn'athel." She closed her eyes again.

"No," said Romarin.

"Kally," said Cahal. "You said something about Romarin and Lachlan."

Kalena grimaced. The *Chi'lan* really had heard everything she said. "I don't know. I asked. He wouldn't tell me."

"Do you remember the words you used?" Cahal asked.

"You mean when I asked him about Romarin?"

"Do you remember the language?"

Kalena's headache went from severe pounding to a roar. "My head hurts," she whimpered.

Cahal put a cup up to her lips. "Drink. It's for the pain."

She sipped the cool liquid which tasted faintly of cinnamon and anise. There was something else in it that made her drowsy and alleviated her headache.

"We had best leave her under the care of Daimhan," Cahal said to Romarin.

The king nodded. "You're right. We're not going to get much from her tonight."

Kalena's eyes fluttered open for a brief moment. "Rhyn'athel said that he has not forgotten your friendship, Cahal." Then the drowsiness took her and she fell into a deep sleep.

Romarin watched as the new *Chi'lan* warrior closed her eyes and her breathing became regular. He turned to Cahal, who was gazing at him with interest. "Why? Why her?"

Cahal shrugged. "Why not? You and I both know she is more than what she seems."

"But she has no power," said Romarin. "Beyond her fighting ability, there is nothing special about her."

"Indeed," said Cahal. "But beyond my fighting ability, there is nothing special about me either."

Romarin frowned. "I didn't mean it that way, old friend."

"No, you did – and it's not the first time I've had to put a son of Rhyn'athel or two in line," Cahal said with a smile.

Romarin chuckled and then looked back at her. "I wish I knew what Rhyn'athel said to her. She had a message for you, but none for me."

Cahal clapped the king on the shoulder. "I'd say you were the topic of conversation."

Romarin nodded, still troubled. "Will she remember any of it?"

Cahal shrugged. "The fact that she knew *Athel'cen* and doesn't remember it now means that she won't remember everything. Rhyn is like that."

"It seems everyone speaks to my father except me."

Cahal shook his head. "Maybe there's a reason; maybe there's not. Maybe it's not your time to speak to him." He glanced over the sleeping *Chi'lan* in the cots, including Lochalan. Daimhan and the other healers had kept the captain drugged to facilitate healing and reduce the pain; consequently he did not even know that his sister lay three rows away.

Romarin stared at the wounded and then turned back to Cahal. "You mentioned earlier about leading a party to find the source of the fireworm attacks."

"I did."

"I want you to draw up a plan and bring it to me within the next fortnight. We need to stop the fireworm attacks here and now."

Chapter Fourteen

"Not another one," Kalena groaned. She was sitting in the king's library, staring at an old leather-bound tome written in what she had come to understand as an indecipherable language.

A week had gone by since Kalena had become *Chi'lan*. Despite her conversation with the warrior god, Kalena soon learned that most of the *Chi'lan* had either outright dismissed her vision as something brought on by the Trials or simply avoided her. Cahal had given her the assignment of analyzing old manuscripts for anything that might lend a clue as to the fireworm attacks.

At first, it had been a relief to get away from the scrutiny of the other *Chi'lan*, but now the work in the library was sheer drudgery – something Kalena did not have the temperament nor the will to do for long. As she stared at the language that swam before her eyes, she grimaced. She would have to call on Eistla again and that was something Kalena had no wish to do.

Kalena glanced over at the *Shara'kai* woman who was busy restacking books Kalena had pulled out earlier in the day. Eistla's back was turned towards her. *Thank the gods*, Kalena thought. Kalena struggled with indecision as she watched the brown and silver striped braid bounce up and down, mocking Kalena like a finger shaking from one side to the other. Eistla's soft body bounced as she stepped down the ladder, her skirt swirling on the slate floors. She turned around and for a moment caught Kalena's gaze with those green-gold eyes. "What are you looking for again?" She pushed her chubby fists into her hips and glared.

"I'm looking for anything written around Nevfaras' time," Kalena said. "Anything that might suggest why the fireworms are attacking."

Eistla wrinkled her nose as if she smelled something bad. "Well, what seems to be the problem?"

"I can't read this book," Kalena said, pushing the book towards the librarian. "It's not *Eleion*. In fact every book you've given me so far isn't *Eleion*."

Eistla frowned and looked at the book. "It's *Athel'cen.*"

"Some good that does me."

"*You* can't read it?"

"No." Kalena gritted her teeth.

"I thought *Chi'lan* would know *Athel'cen.*"

Kalena looked back at the runes. "This *Chi'lan* doesn't."

Eistla tsked and swept up the book. "This book won't help you. It's the harvest accounting ledgers."

"Damn you!" Kalena snarled. She drew herself up to full height – she was a good five inches taller than Eistla and the woman blanched in fear. Although Kalena was not in mail, she was wearing her sword and colors of her position. "I am *Chi'lan* – I am not some child to admonish. I want you to find me anything pertaining to Nevfaras and fireworms. I will be back after dinner to see what you have. If you have nothing for me, I will take this to the king, himself, and you can tell him why you have not assisted me. Is that understood?"

Eistla shrunk back in fear and squawked a terrified affirmation, but Kalena had already turned and stomped out the door.

Kalena followed the castle's corridors to the main hall and out into the bright sunshine of the outer courtyard beyond the castle's main gate. Citadel Heights had long ago been built on one of the foothills of the Shadow Mountains. The castle and keep had been built on the highest point with the main fortifications and curtain walls lower on the hill. Within those main walls were the garrison, main hall and much of the older quarter where mostly shops and the more affluent residents resided. Those who lived there were often nobles or even a few *Chi'lan* who had families.

Beyond the safety of the curtain walls, were residences and a second merchant quarter that had been built up to handle an increasing population despite the fireworm attacks. In this hilly country, land was scarce so the few thanes who owned land beyond that tilled it for crops. There was no wall to protect those outside the city.

Looking down towards the merchant quarter, Kalena could already see that the city of Citadel Heights was alive with merchants hawking their wares. It was noon and the smell of baked bread wafted up to her nostrils, making her mouth water. She had not had much to eat for breakfast and was now thinking about food.

"There you are," Cahal said.

Kalena turned around to see the champion striding towards her in the courtyard. She took a deep breath and stared into the blue sky.

"How does the search go?" Cahal asked.

Kalena shook her head, not looking into the champion's eyes. How could she tell him she had failed him?

"There are a lot of books to go through," Cahal said casually. "How has Eistla been?"

"Awful," Kalena said. "The woman is horrid – I don't know why she's the king's librarian."

Cahal chuckled and Kalena stared at him. He shook his head. "She's been like that since Nevfaras's time."

"She's been alive since Nevfaras?"

Cahal nodded. "I remember when she was hired. Dour woman even then. She was the scribe for most of the history."

"Then, she wrote the *Athel'cen!*" Kalena said. "She knew exactly what I wanted and just kept handing me worthless documents." Cahal chuckled, which only made Kalena angrier. She wheeled on her mentor, shaking her fist. "You could've told me."

Cahal stifled the laughter, his silver eyes glinting merrily. "Kally, Kally, part of the *Chi'lan* way is patience. You know this."

Kalena nodded, chagrined at her reaction to Eistla. She had known the woman was difficult, but it hadn't made it any easier. "I'm sorry," she said at last, looking down at her feet. "I shouldn't have lost my temper with her."

Cahal grinned. "Easy to do – I've lost my temper with her more than once."

Kalena stared at him for a moment in shock, and then, stifled a chuckle. "You sent me to her without a warning?"

He smiled slyly. "I didn't want to prejudice you."

Kalena snorted.

Cahal's expression turned serious. "Kally, Lochalan is awake and asking for you."

Kalena caught her breath. "He is?" She knew Lochalan would've heard about her making *Chi'lan*, but wondered what else he had heard.

Cahal seemed to sense her apprehension and gripped her shoulder. "Kally, he already knows. He's proud of you."

Kalena blinked, her mind whirling with conflicted thoughts. Lochalan had been against her becoming *Chi'lan* and was now proud of her? She didn't know what to think as she followed Cahal to the infirmary where she saw Lochalan lying in one of the beds.

Chapter Fifteen

Kalena didn't flinch when she looked at her brother. Despite the sloughing, dead skin and the stench of charred flesh, she could see that Lochalan was doing better even than the day before, when she had seen him. Even then, he had been in and out of delirium, sometimes calling out hers or one of the other *Chi'lan's* names; sometimes staring at the ceiling, his silver eyes glazed over as though he looked into another world. Kalena had done the best she could to care for him while she was there. But as a *Chi'lan*, she had other duties to perform. Most of those duties had been the library research that confounded her.

Lochalan's silver eyes were no longer glazed over. Instead, they looked lucid and alert as she walked into the infirmary. The skin was peeling off in jagged strips, but she could see the scarred new skin beneath the dead. The new skin was pockmarked and uneven. Lochalan would never be as handsome as he had been.

Kalena shook the thought from her head. Rhyn'athel didn't care what his warriors looked like – the bravery, the honor and the devotion of his warriors mattered more. Even so, it hurt Kalena to see her brother like this.

"Kally." Lochalan's voice was raspy and not much more than a whisper, but she felt she would've heard his voice even across miles. Despite the enormous age difference and despite their quarrels, Kalena could feel the blood-bond between them. Whether she liked it or not, he was indeed her brother.

"Save your strength," she said softly, sitting beside him. "Are you thirsty?" He nodded and she poured a cup of water and pressed it to his lips. They were cracked and bloody, but she held her hand steady.

He waved her hand away. "I heard you made *Chi'lan*."

Kalena nodded. "The last attack took out too many warriors; Romarin was desperate."

Lochalan grunted but Kalena couldn't tell if it was amusement or chagrin. "I can't imagine a better *Chi'lan*."

Kalena felt a lump grow in her throat. "You mean that?"

"Would you doubt the word of your captain?" He tried to smile. "I hear you had a conversation with Rhyn'athel."

Kalena lowered her eyes and shook her head. "I don't know – that's what they say."

"You don't remember?"

"No. I guess it wasn't for me to share." She paused. "Honestly, I don't think I'm special."

"I think you are," Lochalan said. "I know Cahal thinks you are. You might even make champion someday."

Kalena laughed. "Champion. That's the one thing I'm not looking to be."

Lochalan nodded. "So, what is Cahal having you do?"

She snorted. "He's having me go through musty old tomes."

A glint of interest entered Lochalan's eyes. "He has you looking through the Library? What for?"

"For anything that might point us to why the fireworms are attacking."

"But we've done this before. I remember when I became *Chi'lan*, there was a similar search. We turned up nothing then." Lochalan's voice wasn't strained or accusatory. He sounded tired. "Fireworms are quarrelsome beasts, Kally. They're not very smart and look for shiny things to line their nests with. Who knows why they attack? Maybe they just like to kill."

Kalena frowned. "So, you're saying they're not as smart as dragons?"

"No, not at all. Dragons are smart. They can talk to people and have powers beyond what a fireworm has. I don't know how they're related to dragons, but many say the fireworms are ancestors to the dragon. Although it's a good guess, I don't think that's true."

"Would a dragon know why the fireworms attack?"

"Kally..." The alarm in Lochalan's hoarse voice was unmistakable. "Kally, Allarun controls the dragons. If you approach one, it'll be certain death."

"Of course." Kalena hoped her voice didn't sound too brusque, but she knew she had to put her brother's mind at ease. "One would be foolish to seek out a dragon."

Mollified, Lochalan laid back against the pillow. Kalena poured him more water and pressed it against his lips. After which, neither spoke. Kalena continued to sit by his bed as he fell into an uneasy sleep.

As she watched her brother's chest rise and fall with each breath, her mind went back to the problem of why the fireworms were attacking. Most of the *Eleion* seemed to think that it was Allarun's wrath, but Cahal didn't think so. Cahal's instincts were usually correct – they were borne out of over a thousand years of experience. He had been Lachlan's foster father and had been at the great warrior's side when he had died at Allarun's hands. Cahal had known Allarun even before he became the emperor.

Kalena suspected that Cahal had known the dragons before they became Allarun's servants.

She hadn't lied to Lochalan when she told him she didn't remember the conversation with Rhyn'athel, but she did remember speaking to the god. Something told her that the god would guide her actions. And now, she felt as though the god had given her and idea. She just hoped it wouldn't get her killed.

Chapter Sixteen

Kalena returned to the garrison, looking for Cahal. When she didn't find him there, she made her way back to the castle. The dragons. That had to be it.

Her feet found her way up the steps towards the king's throne room. Cahal was most likely with the king. She hesitated at the massive oak doors and the two guards outside. They would let her pass without a second glance because she was *Chi'lan*, even if a newly made one. Still, the thought of what she was about to do caused her to tremble inside. She was going to interrupt the king and the king's champion.

You are Chi'lan, a voice within her spoke. *You have every right to be here.*

Kalena took a deep breath. No, she wasn't a captain like Lochalan nor was she the champion, like Cahal. But she was *Chi'lan* and that put her as an equal to all other *Chi'lan* – even the king. She steeled herself and stepped past the guards, who opened the doors to the throne room.

The room was much as she remembered. Smoky from sconces and dark, it seemed something that no *Chi'lan* would stay in long. Yes, the tapestries were impressive and the room had overwhelmed her when she had first seen it, but now, looking at it, it seemed a cage. A cage for a man who did not wish to be there.

Her mind went back to Romarin and at that moment, she remembered the god's words the promise she made to Rhyn'athel:

"Romarin is my son; that much I will say. But his way is uncertain and he needs someone strong to stand with him in battle. That person is you, Kalena. Until Lachlan returns."

Kalena shivered. *What did this mean?* she asked the god. When she agreed to it, she knew what she had promised; she knew what she had said. Now, it was a blur. She turned and looked at the throne – a massive, oak chair with dragons entwining along the legs and arms. Dragons.

Rhyn'athel's standard had been dragons. The pieces fell into place as she looked around the throne room. On the wall were tapestries with the dragon motif throughout. And one tapestry showed Lachlan, himself, riding a black dragon.

The dragons hadn't always been under Allarun's control – they had been creatures of Rhyn'athel before the emperor had taken control of them. They were still creatures of Rhyn'athel, even if they were forced to obey the emperor. If she could somehow speak to one, somehow gain its knowledge, she might have a chance at figuring out why the fireworms attacked. If it were Allarun, then all hope was indeed gone. There weren't enough troops in Citadel Heights to break the emperor's hold. But, what if it weren't Allarun? What if it were something else?

Kalena considered the tapestries. Lachlan had ridden a dragon. As a son of Rhyn'athel, Lachlan's power had been over the dragons. Why couldn't Romarin summon those same powers? She knew the answer even before the question had formed in her mind. Romarin had no one save Cahal to teach him what powers he had. Without another first-blood to guide him, Romarin's powers were largely untapped. Could Romarin control dragons the way Lachlan had?

She traced the dragon carving along the throne. Dragons; not fireworms. These creatures were smart, cunning and magical. She knew where her answer lay.

"Kalena?" Cahal's voice echoed in the near darkness of the chamber. Kalena turned and felt her face grow hot as she saw Cahal and Romarin standing beside him in the doorway. She was glad the king couldn't see the flush in the dim light.

"I was looking for you," she said, removing her hands from the throne's arms. "It's dragons."

Romarin looked at her, his face unreadable, but Cahal looked confused. "Dragons?"

"They know," Kalena said, her voice growing steadier. "The dragons know why the fireworms attack us."

Cahal frowned. "Kally..."

She shook her head. "No, I'm sure. The dragons would know."

"Then we might as well beg for Allarun's mercy," Romarin said. "The dragons belong to him."

"No," Kalena said. "The dragons belong to Rhyn'athel."

A silence ensued. Kalena could see Romarin's frown deepen as he clenched the silver gauntlet that replaced his right hand. He turned to Cahal and Kalena felt a prickle along the back of her neck.

They're conversing in mindspeak, she suddenly thought. While she could not hear the words, she could sense the conversation between the two men. She saw Cahal nod slowly and turn to leave. She too turned to leave.

"Wait." Romarin's words barked out like an order. Kalena halted, trembling inside as she watched Cahal walk out of the chambers with the doors closing behind him. She wondered if Romarin was angry at Cahal because of her. Would he send his champion away?

"I'm not angry at Cahal," Romarin said, his voice taking a different tenor now, almost gentle. Kalena let her breath escape her lips slowly. "I told him that I wanted to speak to you alone."

She swallowed hard and nodded.

"What did my sire tell you?"

Kalena's eyes widened. "Rhyn'athel?"

"Yes." He had spoken so softly that she could barely hear him. "He has spoken to you, when he does not speak to me."

She swallowed again, feeling her mouth turn to ash. "I-I..." She looked down, feeling the panic well up inside. She started as she felt his left hand gently touch her chin, tracing her jaw line, as light as a feather. She looked up into his silver eyes and was caught. Sad, expressive eyes, weary from too much battle.

"Kalena," his voice was a whisper, almost pleading. Romarin was handsome and at once, she recalled Rhyn'athel's face. The likeness between father and son was uncanny. Romarin was indeed the son of the warrior god. Why did the god choose to talk to her and not to him?

"My king, I..."

"Romarin," he said softly. "Kalena, my name is Romarin."

"Romarin," she repeated. "I can't..."

"You can tell me," he said.

"Rhyn'athel said..." She faltered. "He said you needed someone to stand beside you in battle."

Romarin's brow furrowed deeper. "He did?"

"Yes, he said your path was..." She paused and tried to recall the words. "Unclear."

A silence ensued as she could tell that he was struggling with conflicting feelings. *He's younger than he appears,* she thought suddenly. She had known Romarin was only fifty-two, since Nevfaras had died fifty-four years before, but somehow seeing the king standing before her made her realize how young he actually was – next to older *Chi'lan* like Cahal. In *Eleion* age, he wasn't much older than her, really. The age difference between her and other *Chi'lan* weren't much more. Fireworms had killed too many of the older *Eleion*.

"Am I Lachlan?"

"Rhyn'athel didn't say."

Romarin turned away. Instinctively, she put her hand on his shoulder, and then realizing what she was doing, pulled away. He turned and caught her hand, holding it gently, but firmly in his own. His warm fingers sent a shockwave through her. "Tell me, did Rhyn'athel tell you about the dragons?"

"No," she said softly. "Not directly."

"Not directly." Again the frown. "Do you hear the god speak?"

Kalena shook her head. Did he think she was lying to him? Did he think that somehow she had made up speaking with Rhyn'athel? She slowly met his eyes with her own and realized how close he was to her. How he was holding her hand and looking deeply into her eyes. "The god hasn't chosen me," she said, wanting to tear her gaze from his and finding she could not. "I'm not special, Romarin."

A small smile played across his lips. *Sad*, she thought.

He released her hand and at once she pulled away. Her thoughts were muddied and confused. "You may go, *Chi'lan*."

Kalena stepped backwards, nearly tripping off the dais. He caught her and for a moment, he held her in his strong arms. Her face turned red and he grinned impishly – the first time she had seen him do so. He released her with an embarrassed laugh, and she slipped away and out the doors as fast as she could.

Chapter Seventeen

"He finds you quite beautiful," Cahal said as Kalena drew her sword for sparring.

They stood in one of the many courtyards adjacent to the garrison that was often used for sparring practice and drills. Not much more than an out-of-the-way yard paved with cut stones, it had walls and a gate that afforded some privacy. Cahal stood on one side of the yard while Kalena stood at the other side. They wore their armor – mail hauberk with thick padding underneath and helms that covered the head and bridge of the nose. A mail coif protected their necks beneath the smaller helm. Their legs were unprotected except for the mail skirt that hung split, almost to the knees.

Kalena was now a *Chi'lan* warrior and didn't have to spar with Cahal, but Cahal hadn't taken a new *chi'li'a*, which made her grateful that the old *Chi'lan* saw fit to train with her.

Her mouth hung agape and she nearly dropped her sword. "What?"

Cahal charged with a grin, swinging the long sword, *Fyren*. Kalena barely had time to parry the blow. "Don't drop your guard," he said as he swung the long sword effortlessly.

"That's unfair," she protested.

"Your enemy won't be fair," Cahal chided. "Never lower your guard, no matter what you see or hear."

Kalena grunted as she parried his blow. "*Who* thinks I'm pretty?"

"Who do you think?" Cahal teased. "Romarin, of course."

"Romarin? He's the king." Cahal laughed and took another slash at her. She parried. "What's so funny?" she demanded.

"He's a man, too," Cahal said. "You can't expect to trip and end up in his arms without some stray thoughts."

She could feel her face turn red. "That was an accident." She bellowed and charged him with a flurry of sword blows.

"An opportune one," Cahal said with a grin, backing up. "I didn't realize you were so taken with him."

Kalena broke off and circled Cahal warily. "Taken? I'm not *taken* with him."

"You're not?" Cahal frowned. "Why not?"

Kalena stopped her circling. Sweat was pouring down her face. Despite the cap beneath the coif and her short haircut, a loose strand of hair was being pinched through the mail's links. She felt angry at Cahal and she didn't know why. "He's the king."

"Yes, he is," Cahal agreed. "And you will someday be his champion."

Kalena frowned. "You keep saying that, but *you* are his champion."

"Not forever," Cahal said. "Didn't Rhyn'athel tell you this?"

"Rhyn'athel?" She hesitated. Cahal didn't press his attack, but instead looked at her. "What did Romarin tell you?"

"He told me what Rhyn said to you."

"Rhyn—you mean Rhyn'athel?" She looked at the old *Chi'lan* and smiled. "You were good friends."

"Close friends," Cahal said. "I knew Rhyn'athel first as a fellow *Chi'lan* and then as a brother. He didn't reveal himself until our final battle against Areyn Sehduk."

Kalena blinked and rubbed the sweat from her eyes. She knew Cahal was old, but how old?

As if reading her mind, Cahal sheathed his sword and removed his helm. "Kally, look at me. I am possibly the oldest *Eleion* alive, assuming Laddel and his clan are no longer."

Kalena sheathed her sword and stared. She hadn't really paid much attention to the silver strands that streaked his red-gold hair that had been cropped so short from wearing the helm. She could see now that there were more silver and white hairs than red-gold. His skin wasn't wrinkled like she saw with the *Ansgar* or even the *Shara'kai*, but it looked leathery and worn, as if it had been a parchment taken out often and tattered to the point where the edges were no longer where they should've been. "You're not old…"

Cahal laughed. "You lie poorly, *Chi'lan*. I am over fifteen hundred years old."

Kalena stared. The number was inconceivable to her mind. "Fifteen hundred? Is that possible?"

"Think about it – how could I have known Rhyn'athel? How could've I trained Lachlan and Elsonre? How could I have seen Allarun rise to power?"

"You're—you're immortal?"

"No, Kally, I'm not. I'm like you. It's just we're such a long-lived race if we aren't killed. Maybe godlings like Romarin don't die in age, but I will. My line, like yours, holds no godling blood in it save perhaps Lochvaur's blood. But Lochvaur's blood was thousands of years even before I was born. I am cursed with being a great warrior."

"Cursed?"

"Cursed, in a way. I have outlived all of those I have known when I first became *Chi'lan*. Fialan, Tamar, Lachlei, Kian – all of the *Chi'lan* I knew are no longer in this world. Areyn Sehduk's hand closes over all our eyes at some time. But Rhyn has been unwilling to grant me that – until now."

"You wish for death?"

"No, Kally, I don't wish for death. I wish to return to the Hall of the Gods. That is where my friends are. That is where I belong, beside Rhyn'athel, with those whom I have fought beside over the millennia."

"Rhyn'athel said he remembers your friendship," Kalena mused. "You're like a brother to him."

"And he to me. And that is why I will not be Romarin's champion for much longer."

A tear rolled down her face, but she felt him wipe it away gently with a gauntleted hand. "Kally, you must become the king's champion. That's why I've trained you."

"But Romarin may be Lachlan. He'll need you."

"Romarin may be – or he may not. If he is Lachlan, then Kally, he surely doesn't need me. Not now. And if he's not, he has the best *Chi'lan* I know of by his side." He smiled at her. "Kally, he finds you quite attractive."

She crossed her arms. She hadn't expected this. "Did he tell you that?"

"No, not in so many words, but I've lived long enough to see it in his eyes. He was quite taken aback at his reaction to you." He grinned again. "Did you really just trip?"

She sighed in exasperation. "What do you think?"

He chuckled. "Yes, I suppose it was a mistake. But I've seen you look at him – he is quite handsome."

"He looks like Rhyn'athel," she said.

Cahal raised an eyebrow. "Yes, I imagine he does," he said slowly.

"You don't remember?"

Cahal shook his head. "It was so long ago, Kally. Almost as though it were another lifetime. If I were to see Rhyn again, then yes, I would remember. But I watched Romarin grow up, so that has colored my perception."

Kalena considered his words. "When will you..." Her voice trailed off.

Cahal shook his head. "I don't know, Kally. I don't have the Sight and Romarin cannot see my passage either. I only hope I can solve the problem of the fireworms before I leave."

Kalena nodded.

Chapter Eighteen

Kalena looked around the mead hall later that day. After their workout, she returned to the library once, looking through the dusty tomes. Her angry words to Eistla earlier that week now caused the woman to scurry away from her the moment she entered the room, looking for texts. As Kalena turned to look at the shelves, she caught movement in the corner of her eye. Eistla left a book on the table and fled before Kalena could even thank her.

The book had been a history of the time around Nevfaras' reign. What was more, the writing was in a language she could read – not *Athel'cen*. The words came to life as she read about the fight for the crown between Nevfaras and a *Chi'lan* named Torfar:

After Sitharel's death, two contenders for the crown appeared. One was Nevfaras, son of Sitharel, the king's champion and beloved of Krysa, Ardra's daughter. The youngest son of Ardra, a powerful Chi'lan named Torfar...

Now, she looked for Cahal. The mead hall was mostly empty save for the servants who were preparing the room for the nightly meal. Three tables were being brought out where once over a hundred *Chi'lan* feasted. The room's size dwarfed the tables beside the immense firepit where the servants stacked the wood.

What few *Chi'lan* were in the mead hall, looked at her curiously as she strode in. To her chagrin, Cahal was not there but when she turned to leave, she saw both him and Romarin walking towards the room.

"Cahal," she said and then flushed when she saw that she had interrupted the men's conversation.

"I think it would be best if I led an expedition," Cahal said, finishing the sentence. "The dragons would know why the fireworms attack."

Kalena swallowed hard, trying to contain her excitement. Cahal had thought that her suggestion had merit and was going to find a dragon. *But where?* she wondered.

Before Romarin could answer, Cahal had turned to Kalena. "Have you found something?"

"Maybe," she said, facing Cahal, even though she felt the king's gaze on her. "What do you know about Torfar?" From the corner of her eye, she could see Romarin start. She couldn't help herself and saw mixed emotions in his face. "Who is Torfar?" she asked tentatively. "I've never heard of him sung in the mead hall nor is his name carved into the walls, like all other great *Chi'lan*."

"And you won't," Cahal said grimly. "He was the *Chi'lan* who betrayed Nevfaras."

Kalena took a sharp inward breath, despite herself. "I'm sorry."

"Kally..." Cahal began, but Romarin had raised his gauntleted hand for silence.

"Don't be sorry, Kalena." Romarin's voice was even and his face a mask. "It happened before you were born, and for too long, we have kept the story silent." He paused. "But perhaps it is best you knew it, even though it has nothing to do with the fireworms."

Kalena nodded as he led them into the mead hall. The servants had lit the fire and he motioned them to be seated at a table, while the servants brought mead for all of them. Cahal gave a warning glance to Romarin as the servants filled his flagon.

"I won't be drinking much," Romarin said to Cahal's look. "But I think Kally needs to know about Torfar. He smiled and shook his head. "Many years before I was born, Sitharel, the son of Elsonre, died in a battle against Allarun. He had one son, a *Chi'lan*, my stepfather and namesake, Nevfaras. Nevfaras was a great *Chi'lan*, but unlike many first-bloods, he held no real power save mindspeak and his skill as a warrior. In retrospect, he probably had other powers we didn't know about, but he was not anywhere as gifted as many of the first-bloods usually are.

"But Elsonre had three sons and one daughter. The other two sons died in battle with no heirs. But Elsonre's daughter, Ardra married bore two children, both *Chi'lan*. One was Krysa; the other was Torfar."

"Krysa was easily the better of the two," Cahal interrupted. "I had trained her, just as I have trained you."

Kalena smiled. She recognized the pride in Cahal's voice.

"Torfar, however, was her exact opposite." Cahal continued. "Oh yes, he was *Chi'lan*, but he was quick-tempered and loved the magic arts. His powers were exceptional – he could call the storm wind down from above and create illusions that were beyond anything I've ever seen, other than from a godling. What's more, he was ambitious. He hungered for power. So, when Sitharel died, he naturally assumed the Council would choose him to be king."

Kalena looked from one man to the other. "They didn't, did they? They chose Krysa, right?"

"But Krysa had no desire to be anything other than *Chi'lan*," Romarin said. "She had made it quite clear to Cahal, who was the head of the Council at that time, that she would not be a warrior queen."

"I foolishly respected her wishes," Cahal said. "But she convinced me that she was not to be queen. That is when Nevfaras stepped forward. He had fallen in love with Krysa and sought to win the throne – and her love."

"How romantic," she said. "What did the Council do?"

"Nevfaras was first-blood and *Chi'lan*, but he had no powers," Romarin said. "While a first-blood and having magic is preferred, the *Lochvaur* have had kings and queens without a drop of godling blood in them and without magic. Nevfaras was the Council's choice for king. Torfar challenged him."

"And Nevfaras won?" Kalena asked.

"Nevfaras lost," Cahal said. "But Torfar had used magic to defeat him, so Nevfaras was made king. Nevfaras should have exiled him – it was his right – but Nevfaras loved Krysa and did not wish to lose her love."

"Hatred grew in Torfar's heart over the loss of the crown that he sought to destroy Nevfaras. He entered into a pact with Allarun and betrayed not only Nevfaras but also the *Chi'lan*. Allarun attacked Citadel Heights and after several long sieges, Nevfaras was captured and taken away to Allarun's stronghold, Sehduk's Keep." Romarin paused. "Nevfaras met his end as a sacrifice to the death god."

Kalena shivered. "What happened to Torfar?"

"Torfar disappeared after the battle. I suspect he, too, was sacrificed to the death god because Allarun wouldn't tolerate a first-blood *Lochvaur* – not even a traitorous one who served his purpose," said Cahal. A silence ensued.

"Krysa had married Nevfaras before the battle," Romarin said. "They both seemed to know something was about to happen – maybe the Sight showed them that." He paused. "I was named after Nevfaras in his memory, even though I am the son of the warrior god."

"And Krysa became queen, even though she didn't want it," Cahal said. "When Romarin was born, she knew she had to remain queen at least until Romarin had come of age. Even so, we lost her to battles with Allarun, but the fireworm attacks had already started."

Kalena frowned, considering the story. "There's no relation, then."

"Not unless you can see a relation that I can't," Romarin said. "Torfar could still be alive, but to call down fireworms upon us?"

Kalena nodded slowly, still unsure. "Maybe there's more to the story than we know."

"Perhaps," said Cahal. "In the meantime, I want you to prepare for a journey. Romarin has agreed to let me take a few *Chi'lan* into the mountains in search of a dragon, who might be able to tell us what causes the fireworm attacks."

Chapter Nineteen

Kalena had opened her saddlebags one more time to recheck the contents when she heard a knock on the door. She glanced around her sparsely furnished room – she had laid out the bedroll, canteens and saddlebags across the bed as the only other piece of furniture, the chest, had her armor and weapons strewn across it. She shrugged at the mess and opened the door.

"Kally!" Lochalan grinned and gave her a hug before she could do anything. Kalena found herself laughing with delight as he swung her around off her feet and kissed her on the cheek.

"I thought you'd been in the infirmary for another week," Kalena said when she finally caught her breath. It had been a week since Cahal had told her to prepare for the journey. She looked at Lochalan's face – the scars were an angry, swollen red, but she could tell he was healing.

Lochalan shook his head. "Daimhan proclaimed me fit to go. I think Cahal had something to do with that. I'll be coming with you and Cahal on this little expedition."

"You will?" Kalena couldn't stop the grin crossing her own face. "You're going because you want to order me around, don't you?"

He laughed. "The gods know Cahal can't control you. And I am your superior officer."

"Yes, sir," she sneered. "We'll see how quickly *that* will last."

Lochalan shook his head. "I know. I heard about your trial – how you fought against Elsayr, Cahal and Romarin."

Kalena shrugged. "It was nothing."

"You drew blood on Cahal, and Romarin cheated."

"Lochalan!"

"It's true. Cahal said you would've defeated him if he hadn't used the gauntlet. That gauntlet isn't from this world. It's a deadly weapon in its own right. Romarin can crush adamantine with it."

Kalena's eyes went wide. "Really? Where did he get it?"

Lochalan shook his head. "He's told no one. Not even Cahal – and they're the closest of friends. He's only said that he lost his hand and found another to replace it."

"Hmmm," Kalena mused. "It was when he searched for the Sword of Destiny."

Lochalan nodded. "What I've been trying to say is that you've done as well as anyone – maybe even better. And to garner a god's favor."

"I don't know if I have Rhyn'athel's favor," she said.

"I do." Lochalan paused. "It's almost noon – let's get something to eat. We'll probably not get more than hardtack for weeks."

Kalena chuckled and nodded. She paused to slip her sword belt on before following her brother out the door to the main hall.

As they entered the main hall, the smell of freshly baked breads and salted meats filled her nostrils. Kalena grinned as they sat across from each other and pulled bread, meats and cheese from the platters the servants brought.

"So, you really think a dragon may be able to tell us something?" Lochalan said, once they had settled into eating.

"I think there's a fair chance," Kalena said between mouthfuls of bread and meat. The meat was cold and greasy, but she washed it down with water. "According to what I've read, the dragons are intelligent."

"But aren't they under Allarun's control?"

"Yes, but only when he calls them. Allarun can't control them all the time. If we find one, we might be able to discover who or what is controlling the fireworms."

The peal of a loud bell interrupted their conversation before Lochalan could speak. Kalena's eyes went wide and they both leapt to their feet.

"Fireworm! Fireworm!" The calls came from outside as the lookouts shouted their warning. Kalena leapt up, nearly toppling the table. Swearing bitterly at her clumsiness, she grasped Lochalan by the arm.

"Come on, brother! Fireworms!"

Without pausing to hear Lochalan's terse reply, Kalena ran out of the main hall, joined by other *Chi'lan* warriors and soldiers.

The cold autumn air rushed to greet her as Kalena entered the bailey. Already soldiers and *Chi'lan* filled the streets, looking up for a glimpse of the airborne enemy. Kalena moved away from the throng that was gathering – she couldn't fight a fireworm in close quarters. Instead, she entered a corner tower and climbed the stairs that led to the wall walk, followed by her brother and other *Chi'lan*.

"Did you see it?" Lochalan said, panting as he ran beside her.

"No," Kalena replied. The massive oak door to the wall walk was already flung open and the scene was total chaos. Soldiers and *Chi'lan* were everywhere, rushing to fight an invisible foe or stopping and looking into the skies. Already, men were arming the ballistas with iron-tipped siege arrows and preparing for an onslaught.

Kalena shielded her eyes against the blinding sun to scan the skies for the worm after running her hand through her short-cropped red-gold hair. She had developed a nervous habit of running her fingers through her hair, now that it was cut so short. Kalena silently cursed herself for not putting on her mail.

She gazed into deep blue sky, looking for movement. Could the watch have been wrong? Kalena couldn't imagine such a grievous error even on the part of ordinary soldiers.

The screams ran jolts of fear along her spine. She turned to look at the western cliffs. There it was: black and writhing, its talons clutching the rock nearby.

"The Heights!" she shouted. "Turn the ballistas!"

The soldiers scrambled to turn the heavy siege weapons. Kalena continued to scan the skies. *Was there only one? Fireworms seldom attacked alone...*

"*Chi'lan* Kalena!" came Cahal's voice. Kalena turned to see Cahal, but he was frowning. "Where's your armor?"

"We came from the great hall – we're off duty..." She stammered and her voice trailed off as Cahal scanned the cliffs.

"You know better than that," he said, his voice reproachful and he glared at Lochalan. "Shouldn't you be in the infirmary?"

Lochalan shook his head. "Daimhan said I'm fit for duty."

Kalena could see Cahal didn't quite agree. He turned to Kalena. "Kally, I want you in command of the ballistas on this side of the wall. Lochalan – I need you along the east wall."

Suddenly the fireworm screamed and five others appeared from behind the cliffs, diving towards them, claws outstretched and belching fire. As the fire shot towards her, Kalena ran, knowing well that standing and fighting meant dying. She barely heard the screech above the pounding of her heart in her ears and twisted sideways in time to parry the fireworm's claws. She had no time to think. She rolled away from the deadly, venomous talons and leapt up, plunging her sword into the creature's thin leg.

It screeched and snapped. Kalena barely avoided the dagger-like teeth and the hot sulfurous breath as the creature spouted flames at her.

"Kally!" She heard Lochalan cry from somewhere nearby.

Instinctively, Kalena rolled, barely missing the talons as they came for her again. Another snap and another. All she could see was fireworm coils around her.

She thrust upward with her sword, cutting deep into the worm's belly and eviscerating it. The stench of fireworm guts made her sick and dizzy but she held onto her sword with both hands and kept cutting. The creature thrashed and she pushed aside the coils with all her strength. Stinking and covered with fireworm blood, she stepped away from the dying creature.

"Kally!" Lochalan shouted. He wasn't ten feet from her and pulled the sword from the creature's spine. He was covered with blood as she was. "Are you all right?"

It took Kalena a moment to catch her breath and realize what her brother had done. "Thanks."

"Kally! Lochalan!" Cahal's voice made them turn. Around the king's champion was a dead worm. He pointed to the western cliffs. Fireworms swooped from the craggy rocks above. Kalena could see dozens of fire-worms appear from the cliffs.

"By Rhyn'athel's sword!" Kalena exclaimed. Cahal made no reply.

A large black worm turned in mid air and headed straight for her. Flames issued from maw. Kalena leapt aside, barely escaping the fire. The worm turned again, and another jet of flame shot from its nostrils. Kalena dove and hit the ground hard. She rolled as her cloak burst into flames. She tore the cloak off and leapt to her feet in time to meet the fireworm in its attack.

It snapped at her and she parried the sharp fangs. They dripped with venom. The worm had the speed of a viper as it struck, but Kalena parried again. Its long body whipped around, trying to coil itself around her. Kalena slashed at the exposed underbelly and the worm hissed and screamed. Kalena thrust her broadsword into the softer tissue between the scales. The creature thrashed and then lay still.

Kalena turned. She had no idea where Cahal and Lochalan were. All around her were soldiers and *Chi'lan* fighting fireworms in mass confusion. Blood – both *Eleion* and fireworm – stained the wall walk. She could see the men at the ballistas trying desperately to turn the heavy siege weapons around to fire while the fireworms attacked them. It was a futile effort.

"Damn them!" she snarled, running towards the heavy crossbows. "Forget the ballistas!" she shouted. "Swords out!"

Suddenly, Kalena was clubbed from behind and knocked off her feet. Claws raked down her back, shredding through her clothing. Hot pain shot through her and the worm was on top of her. Kalena rolled, still somehow hanging onto her sword. She kicked and slashed at the fireworm above her. It screamed and sunk its teeth into her shoulder – barely missing her head.

Hot venom poured into Kalena's shoulder and burned as it entered her bloodstream. Pain turned to anger and Kalena slammed her sword pommel against the creature's snout. It let go and with a last effort, Kalena thrust the sword blade backward between the fireworm's scales and into its neck. It thrashed, ripping the sword from her hands. It then collapsed on top of her.

The pain was incredible, but Kalena dragged herself from beneath the fireworm's corpse. Half-blind and choking on blood with each ragged breath, Kalena pulled herself along the wall walk. *The venom*, she realized. It would kill her if she didn't find a healer soon.

The fighting still raged all around her. In her last moments of consciousness, Kalena saw Cahal fighting two fireworms. One worm attacked him while another wrapped its slender body around him. Cahal slashed at the coils, but the fireworms sunk their fangs in.

"Cahal – no!" Kalena gasped, but her words came out as a hoarse croak. Pain overtook her and she fell unconscious and knew no more.

Chapter Twenty

Cold. She was so cold.

Kalena awoke to sunlight. She shivered – she felt as if there were ice in her veins. Kalena opened her eyes, but everything was out of focus. *Am I dead?* she wondered. Kalena was aware of the pain in her shoulder that ran down her arm. She tried to move it.

The pain became excruciating and she nearly cried out. She bolted upright only to have more pain rack her body. Her back began to burn.

"Easy, Kally," came a familiar voice.

"Where in the gods' names am I?" Kalena gasped, her voice raspy. All she could see was blurred light.

"Infirmary," said the voice. "Can you see anything?"

"No – just light. Am I blind?"

"The healers say it's temporary – fireworm venom," the voice said. "Lie back down…"

"No."

"Honestly, Kally…"

Kalena hesitated. "Lochalan?"

"Yes, it's me."

The memory of the battle flooded back. "Cahal – Cahal – he…"

"Take it easy, Kally," Lochalan's voice said. "I'll let them know you're awake."

"What happened to Cahal?" she demanded. Her throat grew tight and she felt a slow, sinking feeling in her stomach.

She could sense Lochalan's hesitation.

"What happened?"

"Cahal's dead," said Lochalan heavily.

Panic seized her. "No, he can't be! He mustn't be! Cahal…"

"Fireworms carried him off." He fell silent for a moment as if trying to sort through the words. "Kally, he's dead. I'm sorry…"

Silence ensued. Kalena felt the hot tears burn down her face. "Oh gods, why?"

"They said he was still fighting the fireworms in mid-air."

"Then, Cahal could still be alive," she said, trying to sit up again. "We must find him!"

"No, Kally," Lochalan warned. "Lay back down. You can't even see. You're not in any condition to look for him, even if he were alive."

"We've got to find him." Silence followed. Kalena paused. "Lochalan?"

"We've already looked, Kally. He's gone." Lochalan paused. "You've been out for a while."

Kalena considered this news. "How long?"

"You nearly died. Romarin had to heal you, himself."

"How long have I been out?"

"Nearly two weeks. There's already talk about replacing Cahal."

Kalena shook her head, trying to comprehend his words. *Two weeks?*

"Listen, you rest. I'll have the healers come by to look at you." He pressed something to her lips, but Kalena tried to bat it away.

"No!" she said.

"It's something for the pain," Lochalan said. "They tell me that it doesn't taste bad. Drink it."

Kalena felt the smooth rim of the cup pressed against her lower lip. She tentatively took a swallow. The liquid tasted vaguely of herbs and fruit, but what it was, she wasn't sure. Kalena nodded as though in approval, and let her brother tilt the cup so she could drink the medicine. As she finished the cup, she began to feel groggy.

"You didn't tell me it had something to make me sleep," she said in accusation.

"You didn't ask," said Lochalan wryly. "I'll let you get some sleep."

Kalena heard Lochalan stand up and walk out, his leather boots making firm strides along the stone floors. She lay back down, her mind whirling with the news. Cahal – dead? Could it even be possible?

Deep down within her, she knew he was gone. The medication made her groggy but did nothing for the pain she was suffering inside. It hurt badly now, so much so that she wanted to cry, only the medicine, the venom and the burns she suffered kept the tears from falling. She was thirsty and tired. She didn't want to think about it any more.

And yet, Cahal knew. He knew he was going to die. Rhyn'athel had granted this terrible wish.

Why, Cahal? We were so close to finding out the truth.

She didn't expect a reply. Her mind went over the terrible fight. How many *Chi'lan* were wounded or killed? How many more would die to the fireworm scourges?

At last, the medication took hold and she fell into an uneasy sleep.

Chapter Twenty-One

The dreams that haunted Kalena were filled with nightmarish visions of fireworms and creatures that looked half man and half fireworm, their teeth sharp and bloody as they feasted on Cahal's remains. Her dream had taken her high up in the Shadow Mountains where the fireworms built their nests and she stood at the cave's entrance as the creatures tore into their bloody prize.

She wanted to scream and run away, but there was no place she could run to. She looked for her sword, only to find herself weaponless. She could not turn away from the horror. The creatures tore huge chunks from Cahal's body. As she stared, Cahal's head turned to her.

Find me, Kally...

The shock woke her up and she jolted nearly upright in her bed. She gasped for breath and thrashed, her blind eyes wide with terror. Someone gripped her, saying something to her and she struggled at first. But as the dream left her, the voice became clearer.

"Kalena?" The deep voice came to her ears, comforting to her. She felt his warm left hand grip hers as she trembled uncontrollably. "Kalena, Kalena. It was a dream. Wake up."

"This isn't the first time," came Daimhan's voice. "It must be the venom having its effect on her."

Romarin spoke again, releasing her as she realized where she was. She was still in the infirmary. And the king was sitting beside her.

Why? she wondered.

"Why, what?" Romarin asked.

Kalena closed her eyes. Did she say this or was he listening to her thoughts again? "I'm sorry," she said, her voice hoarse. She suspected she had been screaming. "Gods, the nightmares. I'm sorry, my king."

"Don't be," Romarin said. "After the fight you've been through."

"Cahal," she said softly. "Cahal spoke to me."

Silenced ensued and she thought Romarin hadn't heard her. Maybe he thought she was crazy. She could hear his breath: slow, measured. "What did he say?"

"For me to find him."

Another silence followed. She wondered if Romarin and the healer were exchanging glances.

"The venom," began Daimhan.

"What?" Kalena said. "Am I crazy?"

"No, Kalena," Romarin said softly. She heard the creak and scrape of the chair legs as he stood up slowly. "If you are, then I am. Get some rest. Daimhan assures me you'll be feeling better in a few days."

Romarin left the infirmary and walked down the hallway. His throat was tight and the feeling of dread filled him. She had dreamed the same dream he had – he was sure of it. This girl who was barely a woman – this *Chi'lan* without first-blood powers or abilities – was receiving the same dreams he had.

It couldn't be a coincidence. Cahal, dead or alive, was telling him and Kalena something important. He wanted Romarin to find him.

Why, Cahal? he asked his old friend. Was it something as simple as bringing peace to the dead? Was it something as terrible as that?

Or was it a clue to why the fireworms attacked? Was Cahal trying to tell them both how to stop the fireworm raids?

Romarin frowned. At one time, before he had lost his hand, he would've gone after Cahal without a second thought. Just as he had searched for *Uruz* and had lost his hand. He wasn't the man everyone thought he was – yes, he was the son of Rhyn'athel, but beyond that, he was little else. He couldn't wield the sword, *Uruz*, and he wasn't the one who would defeat Allarun. And now, he couldn't even save the life of the man who had been his foster-father.

And yet, Kalena was there, dreaming the same dreams. Screaming in horror, just as he had.

Romarin closed his eyes, feeling defeated.

"My king?"

Romarin turned around to see Lochalan looking at him. "Lochalan," he said. "You were Cahal's second-in-command. It's only fitting you become my champion."

Lochalan shook his head. "Romarin, I couldn't take Cahal's place. I was never the warrior he was..."

"You're my best warrior..."

"No, I'm not," Lochalan said. "Kally is."

Silence ensued. Romarin frowned. "You would have me choose her? She's barely a woman."

"We're all young," Lochalan replied. "Few of the *Chi'lan* alive remember Nevfaras – and he was only fifty years ago. The *Chi'lan* are almost extinct save for the few of us who continue. The *Lochvaur* are gone, save you, me and Kally."

Lochalan's words made Romarin swallow hard. It was true. There weren't any other of their kindred left – the other *Lochvaur* had died in the last attack.

"We are the last of the *Lochvaur*." Romarin shook his head. "Perhaps in some ways it is fitting that a son of Rhyn'athel would preside over the death of the *Lochvaur*."

"Perhaps the son of Rhyn'athel isn't here to preside over our deaths, but to issue in a new age," Lochalan said.

Romarin turned around. "Surely, you don't believe I am Lachlan's incarnation?"

"How do you know you're not?"

Romarin smiled grimly, clenching the fist of the silver gauntlet. "I know, Lochalan."

Lochalan gazed at the gauntlet. "You're a son of Rhyn'athel, Lachlan's incarnation or not. The past is past. We must go forward."

Romarin nodded slowly. "Kalena and I are having the same dreams – I'm sure of it."

Lochalan raised an eyebrow and frowned in consternation. "What dreams?"

The king shook his head. "I've seen the cavern where the fireworms tear him apart. He is calling to me to come to him. To find him."

"Why? Surely he is dead by now."

"I don't know where he is. I only know we have to find him."

Chapter Twenty-Two

Daimhan had pressed some medication for her to drink and she drank it willingly. Kalena fell back to sleep, but it was not dreamless. Once again, she found herself in the fireworm cavern, but the creatures were no longer feeding on their grisly prize. In fact, the cave was empty. She looked around in the dark cavern, knowing well that this was a dream because she could see in the pitch-blackness.

Piles of gold coins filled the cavern – along with other shiny things. Kalena looked down at her feet and reached down to touch the coins. Her hand passed through the pile of coins as though it weren't there. She pulled her hand back, shocked at what she saw.

"They like shiny things, don't they?"

Kalena turned and saw Cahal standing beside her, looking down at the gold.

"You're alive!" She reached out to touch Cahal, but her hands slid through him as though he were mist.

He shook his head. "You're not really here and neither am I. I'm here because you must come here, Kally. You must defeat the evil that lurks here."

Kalena stared. "Evil?"

"Listen, I have no time. Find my sword, *Fyren*, and kill the monster in this cave. The attacks will cease."

"Why? How? Where?"

"Torfar." With that, he vanished.

Kalena awoke with a jolt, her eyes staring blankly at what she knew was the ceiling. "Torfar," she muttered. "Torfar..." She frowned. That name was the name of the *Chi'lan* who had betrayed Nevfaras. Could he still be alive and why would she have to kill the evil that lurked there with *Fyren* to stop the attacks? It made no sense.

She wondered if Torfar could somehow be controlling the fireworms. A sharp headache convinced her that she had thought too much for one day and she closed her eyes again.

The next few days of Kalena's recovery went quickly. By the fifth day, she was able to see and even stand up. By the end of the second week since she woke, Kalena was making small forays to the garrison and living quarters.

Kalena raised her chin a little as she walked into the garrison towards the general living quarters. Although dressed in a simple tunic and breeches and not her armor, she was still a warrior – a *Chi'lan* warrior – a warrior among warriors. A wounded one to be certain. Heads turned as she walked in. Many nodded in acknowledgment to her presence.

The normally loud room was now nearly silent. She could sense that the mood among the few *Chi'lan* left was somber. Losing a great warrior like Cahal made many of the warriors grim. Lochalan sat at a table before the firepit, drinking mead with another *Chi'lan* named Taran. Lochalan saw Kalena enter and motioned her to the table.

"You're looking better," Lochalan said as she sat down. "Will the healers let you drink methglyn yet?"

Kalena shook her head. "Interferes too much with the medicine," she said. "But I'll be off the medication soon enough. The healers say my recuperative powers are almost of a first-blood."

Lochalan chuckled. "I didn't see the fight, but I heard you took on two fireworms."

"The second one attacked me from behind," Kalena grumbled. "I was foolish not to watch my back. I was lucky it didn't take my head off."

Taran shook his head. "I saw you fight that worm -- it swooped down on you from the sky. Not many who were attacked that way are alive now." He gave Lochalan a knowing look.

Kalena bit her lip. "Cahal," she said and her voice cracked, betraying her emotions. She quickly turned her head to hide the hot tears as they flowed.

Suddenly, there was a commotion at the main doors. *Chi'lan* and soldiers scrambled to their feet. Kalena looked over and saw Romarin standing in the doorway.

Kalena stood up along with Lochalan and Taran, despite feeling sick. For a brief instant, Romarin's gaze locked with hers and she heard his voice clearly in her head. *Kalena, we need to speak*. As brief as the contact was, he broke it and Kalena suppressed a shiver. He turned his gaze to the warriors around him. He raised his right hand and the murmurs died.

"You may be wondering why I am here," Romarin said without preamble. "As you all are aware, my commander and friend…" Romarin hesitated. The silver eyes steeled. "…Cahal, died three weeks ago. There is no precedent for choosing a commander of the *Chi'lan*, since Cahal held the command for as long as anyone living can remember. For this reason, I am choosing Lochalan as my champion, until another may be found…" He now looked directly at Kalena. He paused. "That is all."

Kalena turned to Lochalan who smiled grimly. She could feel no excitement and no thrill. Only pain.

"You're champion, my brother" she said. "Congratulations." Her tone was flat. She glanced at Romarin, who was already leaving the hall. Cahal had been closest to the king – how could Romarin replace him so quickly? Kalena looked at Lochalan. He didn't look happy – if anything, he looked as though he might become ill.

Kalena felt hurt and betrayed, even if that replacement had been her brother. What right did Romarin have to chose a champion so quickly after Cahal's death? Yes, he was king, but he was *Chi'lan* too. He should have asked his *Chi'lan* first.

Lochalan lowered his head and shook it. "Kally, I don't want it."

"I know," she said, her voice barely a whisper. "Why did he choose so soon?"

"A king needs a champion, Kally."

She swallowed hard. "Yet, so soon."

"I know. I told him I didn't want it."

Kalena stared at him in amazement. "Romarin offered it to you and you refused?"

Lochalan sighed and nodded. "Kally, I could never live up to Cahal's memory."

"But who else could be the king's champion?"

"You could."

Kalena did not meet Lochalan's gaze. She stifled a sob and closed her eyes. "Cahal was the king's champion. I would be but a shadow of his greatness."

She felt Lochalan grip her hand and was struck at once by how rough and calloused his were. So were her hands – the hands of a warrior. She opened her eyes again. "I don't know, Lochalan. But something has to be done. I don't know what."

Chapter Twenty-Three

That night, Kalena walked along the parapets of Citadel Heights. The stars shone brightly in the cold night sky as she slowly made her way up the tower stairs to the wall walk where she had fought the fireworms almost three weeks before. The cold wind bit through her cloak, making her wounds ache, but Kalena forced herself forward. She nodded to the soldiers patrolling the wall. Some soldiers in an attempt to keep warm stood around metal cauldrons or barrels filled with burning embers, the warriors' faces reflected red in the flickering light.

Kalena soon found herself in the same place where she had fought the fireworms. The wall walks and battlements were still stained with the blood – it would take years before elements washed away the final traces of the battle. She gazed at the spot where Cahal stood.

Suddenly, she felt a presence close by. Kalena turned to see a warrior cloaked and hooded, gazing at the same place. She stared at the figure for a moment before turning back around.

"It was there, wasn't it?" the warrior said.

Kalena hesitated. "Yes."

"You were there." It was more of a statement than a question.

Kalena nodded.

The warrior removed the hood. The silver hand flashed in the dim light. Before her stood the king. Romarin motioned her to be silent. "Walk with me a while; it seems we both have some healing to do."

Kalena nodded, not certain what he meant by his words. "Romarin, I..."

"Do you know why I chose Lochalan as my champion?"

"He's a good choice," Kalena said neutrally. She wanted to confront Romarin and yet, she could see in his eyes that he was in as much pain as she was.

"He is, but you're a better choice."

Kalena shrugged noncommittally. "I'm sure you have your reasons."

Romarin grasped her arm and turned her to face him. His grip was stronger than she expected and he gazed at her, his silver eyes steady. "You disagree."

She met his gaze. "I don't think you should've chosen a champion at this time."

Romarin smiled sadly. "I don't want to, but circumstances leave me with little choice." He paused. "Kally, don't you think it pains me to admit that Cahal is dead?"

She remained silent.

"Kally, tell me what you've dreamed."

Kalena swallowed hard. She wanted to pull away, but knew she couldn't. The silver hand was stronger than flesh. "Romarin, I..."

His gaze softened. "Tell me."

Her resolve weakened. There was so much sadness and hope in his eyes, she knew she couldn't refuse. "I dreamt of Cahal in the fireworm den, with fireworms feasting upon him. He begged us to find him."

Romarin released her. "You're not first-blood."

Kalena shook her head.

"And yet, you have the same dream I have had."

She stared wide-eyed at the king. "You dreamed..."

"Yes, Kalena," Romarin said. "I, too, have awakened screaming. Cahal was like a father to me..."

Kalena lowered her head. "I'm sorry. He was the only family I had besides Lochalan."

Romarin nodded. "I know. Cahal spoke highly of you. I suspect he would've had me choose you as my champion..."

"I don't want it – I could never be Cahal."

"I know – that is why I chose Lochalan."

She caught her breath and gazed at the king in wonder. "You chose him because you knew that I wouldn't accept?"

"Yes, at least not now. There's too much pain for us both." He paused. "I had hoped that Cahal would've stayed with us a little while longer, but I guess Rhyn'athel had other plans."

A tear slipped down her cheek and to her surprise, he touched her face gently. "I'm sorry," she said. "I should be stronger than this."

"Kally, you've done more than any warrior your age, except perhaps Lachlan, and you worry about a tear or two? Tears aren't always a sign of weakness." He turned to leave.

"Wait." Kalena's voice came out in a raspy croak. "There's more."

"More?" He turned around.

"Cahal has spoken to me twice."

"Twice? What did he say?"

"He appeared to me as an apparition. He told me we must destroy the evil within the cave if we're to free ourselves from the fireworms."

She could see hope in Romarin's eyes. "What evil?"

Kalena swallowed hard. "Torfar."

Silence ensued. A mixture of emotions crossed Romarin's face. Anger. Rage. Fear. Hope. "The traitor lives?"

Kalena shook her head. "I don't know what it means. Cahal told me we must destroy the evil that sends the fireworms against us. We must find the cave where he died. We must destroy Torfar."

Another silence ensued. "Did you see Torfar in your dream?"

"No. Just Cahal's apparition."

He nodded. "Assuming it was Cahal's apparition."

"You don't believe me?"

He shook his head. "I do believe you. But you're not first-blood. It's unusual for you to have prophetic dreams without the Sight."

"What else could it be?"

"Cahal wasn't first-blood and claimed to have no powers, and yet was capable of mindspeak and other powers we'd normally attribute to a first-blood. The *Lochvaur* were powerful during Lachlan's time – far more powerful than we are."

"I wonder why that is."

"Part of it is blood—over the millennia, we've been hunted to near extinction. The other part is that there has been no one save Cahal who remember the old ways. Most was lost when Lachlan died, what was left was lost with Sitharel, Nevfaras, and Krysa. Cahal remembered much, but couldn't teach what a first-blood could. So, our people have lost their heritage."

"But you're here. You're a son of Rhyn'athel."

"Cahal had powers that he did not tell me about. He taught me what he could, but would often be reticent about his own powers. Probably because he wasn't that powerful among those he knew in earlier times and the powers were unremarkable. Still, he may have powers neither of us know about."

Kalena frowned. "What are you saying? That Cahal somehow left a message for us before he died."

"*If* he died."

Realization dawned on Kalena's face. "Could Cahal still be alive? Even after four weeks?"

"What do you think?" Romarin asked.

"It'd be unlikely."

"Can you think of anyone else who might be able to survive it?"

"Cahal was a great warrior, but four weeks is a long time," Kalena said. "The search parties found nothing."

"The search parties never made it to the fireworm lairs. And even if they did, it would attract too much attention. A few warriors may be able to slip by unnoticed."

Was he going to search for Cahal, himself? "But, you're king."

"Cahal is my friend."

Kalena said nothing. *He hates being powerless*, she thought. *Romarin is the one man who could possibly rescue Cahal.*

"But Cahal may be dead," Kalena said and then immediately regretted it. The haunted look had returned to Romarin's face.

Romarin shook his head. "If Cahal were dead, we must still retrieve the great sword, *Fyren*. Lochvaur, himself, forged that sword nearly five thousand years ago. *Fyren* is not as powerful as the legendary Swords of Destiny, but it is a great blade nonetheless. Cahal told me that Lachlan gave him the blade after forging *Uruz*." He paused noting Kalena's expression. "You've seen the blade, haven't you?"

"Yes," Kalena stammered. "An adamantine long sword -- almost a hand and a half. It has a black stain across the blade."

"You've the good eye for weapons," Romarin remarked. "Not quite a true broadsword, nor a hand and a half. *Fyren* is unique in many ways – like the forger."

"Is it magical?" Kalena asked.

Romarin shrugged. "*Fyren* is forged of good adamantine. Some say that metal came from the world of the gods. It is most likely enchanted, but I never had the chance to wield it. Cahal told me that the stain on the blade is none other than Areyn Sehduk's blood."

"The death god's blood?"

He nodded. "An ancestor of mine, Fialan, stabbed Areyn Sehduk with that very blade before the death god killed him."

Kalena shifted uncomfortably. Did Romarin wish her to seek the blade? She stared at the place where Cahal had stood, as though trying to divine some answer. She turned back to speak to Romarin and found that he was gone ...

Chapter Twenty-Four

"You're going after *what?*" Lochalan exclaimed.

"Shhh!" Kalena hissed, glancing around, her silver eyes nearly steel-gray in the dim light. "Someone might hear you."

Chi'lan warriors, soldiers, and guards filled the mead hall– there wasn't much room and less privacy.

"Who?" Lochalan asked, but much to his credit, he did lower his voice. He looked around. If anyone had heard, he or she didn't bother turning around to acknowledge it. Some of the warriors were repairing and maintaining armor; others, talking among themselves. The low drone from voices blanketed the room, swallowing up Lochalan's outburst.

"Kally, are you crazy?" Lochalan said. "Cahal is dead. If Torfar is behind the attacks, then I can guarantee Cahal died. A traitor like that wouldn't let someone like Cahal live."

"But we don't know what became of him. And he told me, Lochalan, we need to go to the fireworms' lair and kill Torfar."

"Suicide," Lochalan said. "If Torfar is alive; if your dream really is a vision; if you can find the fireworms' lair..."

Her eyes steeled. "I have to try."

"No," he said. "You don't have to try."

She shook her head. "You can't invoke familial rights on a *Chi'lan*, even if you are the king's champion."

"No, I can't," Lochalan said. "But I can order you."

"You wouldn't dare."

"Damn it! We've lost everyone we've known to fireworms," he said. "Kally, you'll be going to your death if you search for Cahal."

"You don't know that."

"You're walking into the fireworms' lairs – if that isn't suicidal, I don't know what is."

"Lochalan, I can take care of myself."

"You nearly got killed fighting in the last attack, Kally, I can't allow you to go on some sort of mad quest because of a few visions."

Kalena slammed her fist against the table. The room became very quiet as she glared at her brother. "It isn't your place to approve or disapprove of my actions, Lochalan," she said in a low tone. "I'll do what I damn well please." Without another word, she stalked out.

It was nearly midnight when Kalena mounted her horse and rode from the gates of Citadel Heights. She had decided to leave while everyone was still in bed to avoid an argument with Lochalan. Kalena felt guilty about her outburst, but she knew she was right. Lochalan was no longer her guardian since she became *Chi'lan* and she certainly didn't need his advice on what to do. She was *Chi'lan* and that meant she was a warrior.

The stars shone brightly overhead in one of the rare moonless nights. Her horse whickered softly as she rode into the dark forest. Ahead of her lay the Shadow Mountains, their dark forms loomed over Citadel Heights' spires.

It had been a long while since Kalena had ridden outside the walls of Citadel Heights. The gloom of the Shadow Mountains weighed oppressive and she half expected to see the dark outline of a winged serpent appear over her. Fireworms were a constant threat, even in the dark forest surrounding Citadel Heights and outlying areas.

Kalena couldn't remember a time when fireworms weren't a threat. She grew up in a small village not far from Citadel Heights. That village was constantly besieged by fireworms. She had lost both her parents when she was very young. If Lochalan hadn't had her brought to Citadel Heights to be raised as a *Chi'lan*, she probably would've languished as another orphan in some dismal town.

Her plan was simple, if a little vague. Cahal had planned to speak to a dragon before he had been killed or captured. She thought that perhaps looking for a dragon might not be a bad idea anyway – it might be able to tell her which way the fireworm lairs were. But finding a dragon was as problematic as finding a fireworm. One didn't really know where their caves were and while Kalena had a good idea where these creatures might be, it could take months or even years before she found a dragon who might talk to her. Assuming it didn't have her for dinner.

In retrospect, Kalena wondered if she had been a bit hasty. She didn't really know the world much outside of Citadel Heights. While she could take care of herself, she wondered what kind of quest she might have gotten herself into. Her confidence waned a bit as the hours passed slowly. She really didn't have a plan or a place to go. Finding Cahal and the sword, *Fyren*, was not much of a plan.

Yet, she continued to ride for hours along the lonely road, watching the steam rise from her breath and from the breath of her mare. The forest was dark and quiet here. The scent of drowsy pine filled her nostrils and once or twice, she nodded on the horse, despite the cold air.

Suddenly, Kalena started awake, listening intently. The forest had grown quieter and foreboding. Just within earshot, she heard it. Hoof beats.

Kalena hesitated. She hadn't been too worried about bandits waylaying her – it was too cold for highwaymen, who would rather spend the night in a warm tavern than work. Anyway, she was *Chi'lan* – most bandits feared the elite *Lochvaur* warriors and avoided the crimson and gold clad surcoats whenever they saw the warriors' colors.

But, with the hoof beats, doubts formed in Kalena's mind. She turned her mare into the forest and rode into the darkness. No sooner had she turned around when a group of six *Chi'lan* soldiers rode past at a quick trot. Kalena watched in surprise.

Kalena waited a few minutes before leaving her hiding place. When she did, she puzzled over what she saw. She decided to trail them to see if they found the fireworm lairs. Maybe Romarin sent them looking for Cahal.

Another thought crept into her mind. Maybe they were looking for her?

She shook her head and chuckled. She doubted Romarin would've sent anyone looking for her and he certainly wouldn't have given Lochalan permission to ride off looking for his wayward sister. Yes, she was a *Chi'lan*, but she knew she wasn't that important in anyone's eyes.

A crimson glow crept into the east. Kalena smiled as she saw the beginnings of dawn. The sun would be a welcomed companion on this journey after six hours under the cold stars.

A scream echoed through the early morning's stillness, pulling Kalena out of her reverie and causing her to rein her horse sharply. She listened. Fireworm! Another scream broke the silence – this time *Eleion*. Somewhere ahead of her, she could make out the sound of a fight. Screams of fireworm mixed with terrified shrieks from horses and yells from men.

"Gods!" Kalena gasped, urging her horse as fast as she could. Kalena's heart pounded in her ears as she realized she might come too late. Suddenly a dark shadow appeared overhead, knocking her from her horse. Kalena fell hard and rolled as the fireworm attacked her horse. The mare shrieked as the fireworm tore into its back and disemboweled it.

Chapter Twenty-Five

Kalena was on her feet and hesitated for a moment as she saw the fireworm feast on her mare. The horse was lost, but the fight was still raging ahead. Kalena drew her sword and sprinted through the dark forest, hoping to arrive before the fireworms could take their prey. The road curved through the dark pinion as she raced ahead and stopped short as she met a gruesome sight.

The air was thick with smoke as flames shot into the sky. The dry timber blazed with worm fire. Kalena saw two *Chi'lan* standing back to back, trying desperately to hold off two fireworms. Their horses were bleeding and thrashing – other warriors' and horses' bodies were charred and strewn across the road. The acrid smell of blood, burnt flesh and hair mingled with the smell of hot fireworm. One *Chi'lan* was noticeably wounded; the other tried desperately to defend them both. A large mature worm of about fifty feet snapped and slashed at the *Chi'lan*. The unwounded man wielded his broadsword, straight at the snout of the creature, slicing deep. The fireworm screamed, shaking its head from side to side. It threw the *Chi'lan* aside like a rag and turned on the wounded man.

With a yell, Kalena charged, brandishing her sword. She leapt into the fray, swinging her broadsword. Its adamantine blade hit the fireworm and cut deep. The worm screamed and turned on Kalena.

:Take my sword! came a voice inside her head. Kalena parried and turned in time to see the wounded man throw a sword towards her. Kalena caught it – just barely and whirled around with both swords, cutting anything that dared oppose her. The worm collapsed in a smoldering heap.

The second fireworm – a smaller creature only half the size of its partner – snapped at her. Swords flashing, Kalena parried and attacked. Fire issued from the worm's maw. Kalena had no time to dodge. She raised her hands up as if to shield herself.

The flames never came. The flames skirted around her as though she had put up an invisible barrier. With a final effort, she wielded her swords and killed the fireworm.

Screams from the fireworm Kalena had left dining on her horse reached her ears. She sheathed her sword, while still holding the other's *Chi'lan's* sword and ran towards the two men. The wounded man looked up. In the dawn's light, Kalena stared into the face of Romarin, the king.

"By Rhyn'athel's sword!" she growled. "Take my hand."

Romarin let her help him to his feet. A terrible gash ran down the side of his leg. He looked down at his own wounds and touched them. The bleeding stopped and the skin closed. "Are you all right?"

Kalena hesitated. "The fire – you stopped the fireworm's flame…" She faltered. *Of course he could do it*, she reminded herself. *He's first-blood…* She handed his sword back.

Romarin shook his head as he sheathed the blade. "I couldn't save them," he said motioning to the charred bodies. "The first attack surprised us and I couldn't get the shield up in time." His face became grim as his eyed the fallen *Chi'lan* who had tried to save him. "Check Lochalan."

Kalena turned in shock. The man whom she had seen the fireworm fling away was none other than her brother. Kalena knelt beside the man and felt his wrist. It was cold and no matter how hard she tried, Kalena couldn't feel a pulse. His head lolled at an odd angle – he had snapped his neck when he hit the ground.

A scream echoed through the forest.

"How is he?" Romarin asked.

Kalena blinked back the tears and bowed her head. "Lochalan," she whispered. "Gods, why did it have to be you?" She turned his head and gazed into the unseeing silver eyes, already glazed over in death.

"Kalena?" Romarin asked.

Bewilderment and anger filled her. "What was Lochalan doing here?" she demanded. "What are *you* doing here?'

"Lochalan was looking for you," Romarin said. "He came to me when he discovered you were gone and I knew you had gone after Torfar. I decided to come with him." He walked over and knelt beside her brother's body. Kalena knew even before he searched for a pulse that the gesture was futile. Romarin looked up. "I'm sorry."

"You can't do anything for him." It was more a statement than a question.

Romarin shook his head. "Not once he crossed the threshold. The first-blood are gifted, but we can't restore a life…"

"Why?" she demanded. "Why was he looking for me?" Her voice was filled with pain and rage. "Lochalan..." She collapsed beside her brother's body and wept. "Damn it, this is my fault. This is all my fault."

"Kally..."

Kalena did not hear Romarin's words. She was shocked and horrified that Lochalan would've come after her – and would've dragged the king into this. She glanced at the bodies of the dead *Chi'lan* – burnt and blackened beyond recognition. She was guilty of their deaths too.

Another scream interrupted her thoughts and echoed through the forest.

She felt a hand touch her shoulder and looked up. "Kally, I know you wish to grieve," Romarin said. "But we're in great danger."

"A pyre," she whispered, remembering Lochalan's words. She couldn't allow his body to be scavenged or rot in the dirt.

"There's no time..." Romarin said, looking around. "We might be able to cover the body with stones once we're out of here."

"A pyre," Kalena repeated. "He is *Chi'lan.*"

"Kally," Romarin said, his voice with an edge to it. "The fireworms will kill us if we do."

"Then I die!" she snapped. "Go back to Citadel Heights and let me build a pyre for my brother."

Romarin looked around. Although the smoke was thick, the fire from the worms had burned itself out. Much to Kalena's surprise, the king knelt down and picked up Lochalan, hoisting her brother's body over his shoulders. "Lochalan gave his life to save me. May Rhyn'athel forgive my folly for this."

Another scream, this time much closer, echoed through the forest.

"We have to leave, now!" Romarin said. No sooner had he said it than a fireworm came crashing through the trees into view.

Chapter Twenty-Six

The fireworm was larger than most and its hide glittered in the early morning sun and smoke. It screamed as it searched for them, but its sense of smell was foiled by the very smoke it and the other fireworms had created.

"Make for the trees," Kalena shouted. "It's our only chance for cover." She drew her sword, backing up and keeping her eyes on the worm as they both ran into the smoldering pines. Another scream and a dark shadow passed overhead. Kalena hoped that the smoke would provide enough cover.

Romarin paused and then turned northward. *:This way!* she heard his voice in her head. She followed Romarin towards some rocky crags. The ground was rough, covered with scree and pine needles. More than once, Romarin stumbled with his burden. He led her to a small fissure within one of the rocky crags. There was barely room for them to crawl into it. Kalena crawled forward and found she could barely fit comfortably if she sat and tucked her knees to her chest. She looked at Romarin, who had laid Lochalan's body outside under some dead branches and barely managed to squirm into the crevasse. His massive six-foot and a half frame made it nearly impossible for him to fit.

"Sorry about the accommodations," Romarin said.

Another screech silenced them both and they waited.

:How many attacked you? Romarin asked.

Kalena met the king's gaze. *:That worm must be the one that attacked me,* she replied with some effort. Mindspeak was difficult for those not born with gods' blood. *:I think there are two.*

Romarin gave the mental equivalent of a nod – she felt a small mental nudge in acknowledgment.

They sat on the cold, wet stone for over an hour, waiting for the fireworms to leave. Once, Kalena thought the smell of her brother's body might lure a fireworm, but the smoke in the air masked the stench. Eventually, Romarin moved stiffly and crawled from the crevice.

"It's safe now – at least for the time being," he said, stretching slowly.

"Are you sure?" she asked tentatively.

Romarin's eyes went glassy for a moment. "They're gone."

Kalena crawled from their hiding place and rubbed her legs to restore circulation. "You wouldn't by any chance have any food or water on you?" The smoke stung her eyes and made her throat raspy.

Romarin shook his head. "I'm afraid all our provisions are along the road, if they exist at all. No doubt the fireworms have gotten to them."

Kalena sighed. "I suspected as much." She turned and her gaze fell on Lochalan's body.

"I'm sorry about your brother," Romarin said softly. He turned to gather wood, leaving Kalena alone in her grief.

It was nearly evening when the pyre was finally finished. They lay Lochalan's body across the boughs and waited for the sky to darken. As the first stars shown overhead, Kalena watched silently as Romarin thrust the torch into the pyre. The dry wood crackled and burst into flames.

Kalena stared at the pyre. Acrid smoke filled the air and stung her eyes and lungs. Tears were gone now, replaced by anger. She clenched her fists. "By the gods," she whispered. "Lochalan shouldn't have died."

Romarin turned towards her and gripped her shoulder in an attempt to comfort her. "No," he said. "I wish I could've foreseen it, but even those with the Sight can't see everything."

Kalena shook her head. "I don't blame you. This was my fault. I left my post to find Cahal."

"No, this isn't your fault," Romarin replied. "Perhaps if I hadn't spoken to you last night, you might not have left."

"But my brother wouldn't have sought you," Kalena mused. "A tempting thought, but not realistic." She paused. "Am I under arrest?"

"Arrest?" Romarin stared at her for a moment and then shook his head. "Who is left to enforce it? Even if I wanted to, what would be the point?"

Kalena sighed. "If Lochalan didn't die here perhaps he would've died in another cursed fireworm raid."

"You believe this?"

"How could I not?" Kalena said. "The *Chi'lan* are no longer the greatest warriors. The fireworms feast on us like prey. Soon there'll be no defenders for Citadel Heights or the king."

Romarin nodded. "And that is why we're both here. To put an end to this one way or another."

Kalena sank to her heels, letting the tears fall. She didn't care anymore if the king saw her weakness. She was too tired and filled with too much grief. "I don't think we can."

"Cahal did."

"Cahal is dead." Her voice was flat. "Cahal thought he knew something, but maybe he did or didn't." She stared at the flames as they began to dwindle. She felt tired.

"What about Torfar?"

"What about him?" Kalena continued staring at the pyre. The flames had consumed Lochalan's body and she now wished for nothing more than to return home. But what was home anymore? The two people she cared about were now gone.

"Cahal told you to kill Torfar."

She sat back on the ground, not caring if the morning's dampness seeped through the mail and arming shirt. She hugged her knees. "I don't know what Cahal told me. I don't even know if the dream was Cahal..."

Romarin knelt beside her. "Kally, do you want Lochalan to have died in vain?"

Kalena blinked back her tears. "No."

"Then, we need to find Torfar. I'm guessing that we'll find a dragon cave if we head northward long enough."

Kalena shook her head. "I'm going back."

"You are?" He looked disappointed. "I can see why. Tell Falar and the others I'm going ahead." He gripped her arms in the tradition *Chi'lan* greeting. "May Rhyn'athel guide your sword." He stood up and began walking.

Kalena stared. "Wait!" she said and Romarin stopped. "Where are you going?"

Romarin turned around. "To find Torfar and maybe Cahal."

"But you're going alone."

"I have traveled alone before."

Kalena shook her head in disbelief. "Not while there's a *Chi'lan* warrior here."

"You made your choice," Romarin said. "I've made mine."

"But you can't..." She fell silent.

"I can't?" Romarin repeated, amused. "Are you telling your king what he can or can't do?"

Kalena shook her head. "That's not what I meant."

"What did you mean?" Romarin asked wryly. "That you thought I would leave my quest to find my best friend, be he alive or dead because I lost my *Chi'lan* guard? That I should give up so readily because this isn't something a king does? Need I remind you that I too am a *Chi'lan*?"

"No," she said ruefully. "What I meant is that as long as I'm here, my duty is to protect you."

"I don't hold you to it," Romarin said turning around and beginning to walk.

"No, but my oath as a *Chi'lan* does," Kalena replied. She caught up next to him. "As long as I breathe, it is my duty to protect the king."

Romarin chuckled and shook his head. "Very well, *Chi'lan* Kalena. I will accept your service."

Chapter Twenty-Seven

They returned to the road to find little salvageable from the fight that morning, but Kalena found a couple of canteens still full of water and a pack with some food. She found one bow intact and three quivers of arrows. Although Kalena could have easily carried the equipment, Romarin insisted that she divide the load equally between them.

She grinned wryly as he shouldered the canteen and distributed the crushed food equally. Despite herself, she found she liked Romarin quite a bit. He was quick to drop the formalities and treated her more as an equal than a servant. She caught herself more than once looking at him idly as he helped her scavenge the pack along the road. But each time he looked up, she quickly looked away and felt her face flush slightly.

Romarin held up one of the quivers. "I'm loathed to leaving any arrows behind, because we might need them. How good are you with a bow?"

Kalena shrugged. "Cahal said I was quite good."

"All right. You should carry the bow and a quiver. I'll carry the extra quiver and we'll try to divide the third quiver between the two so we don't have to carry two extra. It'll make it harder to draw an arrow, though."

"From the looks of the attack, unless I carry a drawn bow, it's not going to be much use anyway," Kalena remarked. "The fireworms are too fast." Once again, she replayed her brother's death in her mind and fought the tears. She wondered what Lochalan would think of her reaction. "How far are we going to have to walk?" she mused, forcing herself to think of her duty rather than his death.

"I don't know," Romarin said. He pointed to the cliffs that loomed in the distance. "The last time I spoke to a dragon, it was over in that range."

"A dragon?" Kalena said, her voice squeaking a bit. "You talked to a dragon before?"

Romarin grinned. "Not all dragons are under Allarun's control. A few are still free." He pointed to the crest on her tattered surcoat. "Do you know why we have a black dragon on our surcoats?"

"It's Rhyn'athel's mark," Kalena said.

Romarin nodded. "Over fifteen hundred years ago, Rhyn'athel freed the *Fyr*-dragons from the eternal fire of creation and destruction. They swore undying loyalty to him."

"But Allarun controls the dragons."

"Not entirely and not all of them," Romarin said. "We may be able to find a few of the most powerful *Fyr*-dragons who have not succumbed to Allarun's magic. If we do, we may be able to talk with one."

"But those mountains are so far away," she said.

"Indeed. I was hoping that perhaps we might reach a village by then and purchase a few horses." He pulled a pouch from the saddlebag. "I wasn't expecting to buy horses, but it'll be enough."

Kalena nodded. It would still be a long walk.

It was late afternoon when they finished scavenging what they could and headed northward. They walked towards the gray bluffs that loomed in the distance. Romarin didn't want to take the chance of being caught in the open in the daytime, since the fireworms had made one such attack, so they stayed in the forest alongside the road. The afternoon shadows grew long and quickly slipped them into twilight.

They didn't speak much to each other, so Kalena was alone with her thoughts and her grief. In such a short time, she had lost Cahal and Lochalan to fireworms. She knew she should feel more pain, and yet, she felt numb. Her tears were gone now, replaced by utter certainty that she had to help Romarin find the reason for the fireworm's attacks. If Torfar were behind the fireworm attacks. She wasn't sure, but what she was certain of was that if there were to be any more *Chi'lan*, she and Romarin had to stop the attacks.

Despite their weariness, they pressed on. Screams echoed overhead twice that evening. Both times, they sought cover, hoping the creatures wouldn't see them in the shadows. They rationed their food, leaving Kalena hungry as they walked. The fight had used up a good portion of her energy and she lay an arrow on the bowstring in the hopes of catching something unawares. While the pile heads were made for piercing mail and cutting into fireworm hide, they would do a passable job taking down a deer or even a rabbit. But the forest was silent and nothing moved.

If Romarin noticed the stillness, he said nothing. Instead, he walked beside her with a confidence she assume came from knowing this land.

Still, the silence of the forest gnawed on her much the same way her hunger did. The road continued northward – in some places, it was a little more than a footpath. Two of the three moons crested the horizon. She frowned as she gazed at the slivered orbs.

"Can we stop?" she said aloud, surprised at hearing the hoarseness of her own voice. Her legs were aching now and she was very hungry. She had only a piece of hard tack since the morning.

Romarin halted and turned to her. "Are you all right?"

"Yes," she said. "Just tired. We've been walking all day and I haven't seen a single animal in all this time."

"You noticed that too?"

Kalena had been kneading the backs of her sore legs and looked up in consternation. "Do you think we're in danger?"

"I don't know," Romarin admitted. "I'd feel better if we moved to a place where the animals are not as reclusive."

Kalena nodded. "That could take all night, though." She paused. "I thought you said there was a settlement or village."

He frowned. "There was, but that was over twenty years ago. The forest has changed quite a bit in that time."

"A settlement could've disappeared, if it weren't that large," mused Kalena. "Even if fireworms didn't attack it."

Romarin uncorked the canteen he carried and drank some water. He shook the canteen and the water sloshed against the sides. The hollow sound told Kalena he hadn't much left. "Let's look for water. We can go several days without food, but we'll die without water."

Kalena nodded. "We're likely to see animals at a stream too."

The sky in the east was growing lighter now and Kalena knew they would soon have to seek cover to avoid fireworm attacks. Water proved to be easier to find – she had found a small ravine that led to a stream where they filled their canteens. Despite Kalena's optimism, they saw no wildlife. The water was clear and cold, running down from the gray cliffs in the distance. Looking in the stream, Kalena saw no fish either. She frowned. She was hoping for something to eat. Most of the vegetation she didn't recognize or trust.

"Why do you suppose there are no animals?" Kalena asked. She dipped her hands in the water – it was icy cold and caused her to shiver. Still, she splashed her face with it and washed her hands.

Romarin said nothing. As she looked up, she saw his hands and the canteens glow for a moment before handing her canteen back. "The water will be safe enough to drink."

"That's handy," she said. "I wasn't looking forward to a case of dysentery."

"I doubt we would get any – there aren't any animals here," Romarin remarked. "I have some *liraya* root that Daimhan gave me, but all the same, I'd rather not use it."

Kalena nodded. She unstrung the bow and rested it against the tree before pulling out the hard tack. "I hate this stuff." She bit into the tasteless biscuit and followed it down with a mouthful of water.

"As do I." Romarin pulled a broken biscuit from his pack and chewed thoughtfully. "I've been thinking about Torfar. It would be unlike Allarun to let Torfar live, which is why I find your dream puzzling."

"Maybe it was just a dream." Kalena shrugged. "We can't discount that possibility."

"Normally I would consider that, especially because you're not a first-blood. But I have had the same first dream and I know the difference between a Wyrd-dream and one that is just a dream. Kalena, you're special. So special that Rhyn'athel spoke to you."

Kalena looked away, hoping to hide her embarrassment from his scrutiny. "Honestly, I remember little."

"But you remember enough?"

"I've told you what I remember." She wondered where he was going with this.

"What did he look like?"

The question caught Kalena off guard. She blinked at him. "Rhyn'athel?" She cocked her head and grinned wryly. "You look just like him."

"Do I?" Romarin didn't mask the curiosity in his voice.

"Oh yes, he's quite handsome..." No sooner were the words out of her mouth that she flushed. She stood up and turned away. "I'm sorry, I...."

Romarin laughed and Kalena chuckled too, despite her embarrassment. Romarin's grin was rakish. "So, you find me handsome?"

Kalena was about to speak when a shadow passed overhead. A scream, not thin and high-pitched as a fireworm's, but not quite unlike it, shook the ground and the trees around them. Kalena fought the urge to throw her hands over her ears. Instead, she ran to the bow and grasped it to string it. Romarin was right behind her and grasped her arm, dragging her into the forest. He pushed her under the boughs before throwing himself against her. His body pressed her hard into the rough branches and bark of the pine.

"What is it?" she gasped as she felt blood trickle down her face as a branch scraped it.

"Shh!" he said. He scanned the skies. "Dragons."

Chapter Twenty-Eight

Kalena caught her breath as she heard the dragon scream again. Despite holding the bow and being held by Romarin, she found herself trembling at the sound. It was worse than any fireworm screech and reverberated through her very bones. She fought the urge to flee, despite the panic welling in her. Another roar – this time almost deafening. Romarin's grip tightened to the point of painful.

What was she thinking when she told Romarin that they should speak to a dragon? A dragon? She looked up and could partially see the beast as it circled over them. It was bigger than she could possibly imagine. While the fireworms were thirty to fifty feet, she guessed that the dragon had to be well over one hundred feet.

:*Why are you here?* The voice seared into her brain. It was angry and strong. :*Who are you? This is my domain.*

Kalena felt Romarin straighten in his stance. :*I am Romarin Nevfaras, son of Rhyn'athel, last of the line of Elsonre Ah'rhyn. I seek Haegl...*

:*Haegl has returned to the Neversummer Mountains where he sleeps. You are trespassing, son of Rhyn'athel.*

Kalena felt Romarin's sharp inward breath. *Did Romarin know a dragon named Haegl?* she wondered.

:*Very well, but I need your aid.*

Silence followed and Kalena could only hear the rasps of their breaths. For a moment, she thought the dragon had left. She glanced at Romarin, whose face was grim. He was scanning the skies.

Another roar and a rush of wind so loud it tore them from the tree's branches and threw them both to the ground. Romarin released her and sprang to his feet, sword in hand. She scrambled to her feet as well, this time stringing the bow and nocking an arrow. Amazingly, the bow hadn't broken in their fall or in their rush to take cover. She steadied her hands and held the bow low, ready to bring up and fire in a moment.

The dragon landed, smashing the trees around it, snapping and splintering them like twigs. It was black with glowing red eyes and scales each the size of Kalena's fist. A row of sharp spines ran down the back, ending in a pointed tail and it beat its massive, bat-like wings bringing up clouds of dirt and debris in a choking windstorm. Kalena shielded her eyes the best she could, but the air was thick and she coughed uncontrollably, despite her attempts to stop it. The air smelled of brimstone.

The dragon turned its enormous head and exposed its sharp teeth. Its head was armored with thick bony plates and sharp ridge horns that ended in points. The teeth were as big as swords. Kalena couldn't imagine the fireworms were the ancestors to these terrifying creatures, despite their similarities.

:*Keep your bow ready*, Romarin said to her in mindspeak. :*I don't want to fight it, but if we have no choice...* She marveled at the king's apparent calmness. Romarin took a few steps forward, still keeping his sword drawn.

:*Stand where you are, son of Rhyn'athel,* the dragon said. Its red eyes had pupils that were slitted like those of a cat. They had narrowed to dark slits in the red irises as its gaze had fallen on Romarin's sword. Kalena marveled. Could the dragon be afraid of Romarin? The idea seemed ludicrous and yet, the dragon was staring at his blade. :*Leave my lands. I have no quarrel with you.*

:*I've come seeking knowledge,* Romarin said. :*I am calling upon my right as Rhyn'athel's heir for your aid.*

The dragon snarled and breathed flames, starting a small forest fire, but it did not approach Romarin. :*I will listen, son of Rhyn'athel.*

:*For over fifty years the fireworms have attacked us,* Romarin said. :*Why?*

A silence ensued as the dragon said nothing. Jets of smoke billowed from its nostrils and it considered Romarin thoughtfully. Kalena frowned, thinking the dragon hadn't heard his words. Then, a single word: : *Nevfaras.*

:*Nevfaras?* Romarin repeated. :*What does Nevfaras have to do with this? He is dead, betrayed by one of our own.*

:*Not one of your own,* the dragon replied. :*Torfar is no longer Lochvaur.*

"Torfar lives?" Kalena gasped, forgetting herself. As the dragon's gaze fell on her, she fought the urge to flee.

:*Torfar lives,* the dragon said. :*Though one could hardly call his existence living. He has been consumed by the very hatred that caused him to betray his people.*

:*We are seeking an old friend of mine, Cahal,* Romarin said. :*The fireworms took him.*

:*Cahal is dead and all you will find there is death*, the dragon said. :*Return to your kingdom, son of Rhyn'athel. Your death awaits you if you continue further.*

"Thanks for the advice," Romarin muttered under his breath. Kalena almost chuckled, despite the fearsome creature before them. :*I can't do that*, he said. :*The worms have destroyed nearly all the Chi'lan. I will not suffer another death, unless it is my own.*

:*And is the Chi'lan with you willing to share that fate?*

There was silence as both looked at her.

Kalena bit her lip and steeled her eyes. "I am not afraid to die, if it means ending this plague."

As she stared into the dragon's eyes, she felt a hard mental push. Instinctively, she raised the bow, but suddenly felt Romarin's hand push her arm down. The dragon grinned, showing all its teeth in a frightening display.

:*Very well, Romarin. I will lead you to the fireworms*, the dragon said.

Chapter Twenty-Nine

Kalena blinked and stared at the dragon. "What?"

Romarin grinned and sheathed his sword. "She's agreed to help us. Put your bow away."

Kalena took in a sharp inward breath. "Why? What does it gain by helping us?"

:*I gain you leaving my territory*, the dragon remarked. :*I'm not fond of visitors. And there is still the small matter of the Fyr-dragons' oath.*

"Fyr-dragons' oath?" Kalena repeated.

"The oath to Rhyn'athel," Romarin said. "For freeing them."

Kalena looked in wonder at the creature. It could easily incinerate both of them with flames if it wanted to, and yet it stood waiting patiently before them. With some misgivings, she put the arrow back in its quiver and unstrung the bow. As she did so, she noticed Romarin was staring intently at the dragon. The dragon was staring back, but neither action appeared to be threatening. The dragon's pupils had widened and it did not fix its gaze hard on Romarin. Romarin's face had softened too. Kalena could see his jaw muscles twitch as though he wanted to speak words.

He's talking to it in mindspeak, she realized. She felt a pang of something – jealousy? – as she realized she wasn't privy to that conversation. Of course she wouldn't be. She wasn't a first-blood and had no real talent, she thought bitterly. Even so, she remembered Cahal hadn't been first-blood and yet could mindspeak well. What's more, he considered the warrior god his closest friend.

Instead, she lay her packs down and started rummaging through them for something to wipe the blood from her face and to make certain she had everything she needed. She pulled her heavier gauntlets back on, looking at the dragon spines and thinking she'd need protection against them and the heat of the dragon's body.

She felt a light touch on her shoulder and looked up to see Romarin standing over her. "Are you ready? Othala says she is."

"Othala?" Kalena repeated. She blinked at the dragon. "She's a female?" As soon as she said that, she flushed.

"I would've thought you'd know the difference," Romarin said chuckling. Kalena could feel herself turn redder.

"To be honest with you, I wasn't exactly looking there," Kalena said. "I'm surprised you did."

Now Romarin turned red. "Actually, she told me," he admitted. "Come on, let's go."

Climbing onto a dragon proved somewhat problematical, but Romarin seemed to be familiar with the procedure. He had Othala bend a leg so he could scramble up the hide and then grasp the scales to pull himself up to just in front of the dragon's withers. There was a space right before the wings where the spines were far apart enough to sit comfortably. Romarin has hoisted himself into the forward spot and offered Kalena a hand up.

Kalena approached the dragon hesitantly. The dragon radiated heat, like a hot fire, and Kalena fought the urge to back away. She climbed up first on the dragon's leg, feeling the heat from even beneath her boots and heavy gauntlets. Othala was heavily muscled and Kalena marveled at the dragon's strength and beauty. She placed her hand on one of the scales and was amazed at the smoothness – so much like glass and yet tougher than almost anything.

"Is everything all right?" Romarin asked.

Kalena smiled up at him. "I'm sorry; she's just so – beautiful."

Othala turned her head at the remark. :*Don't rush her, son of Rhyn'athel. If she wishes to admire me, she can take all the time she wants.*

Romarin laughed and Kalena chuckled too. "I think you've made a friend," he said.

"Indeed," Kalena agreed and hoisted herself up by grasping several scales until she reached Romarin's proffered hand. Her hand slid into the palm of his gauntleted hand and he pulled her up with very little effort. "You've ridden dragons before." She slipped behind him with ease.

"Indeed, I have, when I was much younger," Romarin admitted.

Kalena nodded, gazing at the gauntlet. She knew that was when he had lost his hand. *Could he have lost it while riding dragons? she wondered.*

:*Hold on*, said Othala. She stepped through the broken and smashed trees to get a running start. She then turned around and with a couple of lopes, bounded into the sky.

Wind rushed over Kalena as she felt the dragon's muscles move beneath them. The clawed feet grasped the ground as they pounded hard against the earth before the dragon leapt into the air. It was exhilarating and terrifying all at the same time. The heat from the dragon was nearly intolerable but the wind as it rushed by cooled her. The land fell away in a dizzying swirl of color. Kalena gasped as she looked down.

:*It takes a bit of getting used to*, Romarin said in mindspeak.

That, Kalena could believe. The dragon banked slowly and she gripped harder, hoping she wouldn't fall off.

:*You won't fall off,* Romarin assured her. :*You can relax your grip a little.*

Kalena looked down and to her surprise, found herself gripping Romarin tightly. She knew her face was already red with the windburn, so even if he looked back at her, he wouldn't be able to tell she was blushing. :*Sorry*, she thought in mindspeak. :*I'm not used to this.*

:*You're doing quite well*, Othala's voice broke into the conversation.

:*Where are we going?* Kalena asked. It was difficult to form the mind-spoken words, but she found if she concentrated, she could do it.

:*Othala tells me that the fireworms come from mountains not far from Thalarmor*, Romarin replied. :*They're just within the Lochvaren Mountains.*

:*That's close to Allarun*, she said.

Romarin gave her a mental acknowledgment.

Chapter Thirty

The dragon flew for hours, her strong wings making powerful strokes within the air. They flew northward towards the territory Romarin had said was fireworm domain. The air was cold here and Kalena was glad the dragon was so warm. She was tired and despite the dizzying ride, she found herself nodding off and leaned against Romarin, her arms still around his waist.

A few times, she jolted awake, gripping Romarin in a death-grip as she stared at the rushing land beneath her. None of the land seemed real from here. She was higher than she had ever been on any mountaintop.

Morning turned to afternoon and Kalena was very hungry. She didn't want to risk getting any more hardtack from the pack for fear of falling off the dragon. But as she felt the pangs of hunger rumble in her stomach, Othala had turned.

:*Hold on!* the dragon said.

That was all the warning she gave them. She twisted in mid-air and dove towards the forest below. Before Kalena could catch her breath, she saw a moose galloping through the forest in utter terror.

:*Get down!* Romarin shouted in mindspeak and laid himself flat against the dragon's spine. Kalena lay against Romarin and held on tightly as the wind rushed by at alarming speed. Then, a sudden, bone-jarring impact and a scream. The moose squealed in terror as the dragon pounced on it. Even with all the jarring and shaking, Kalena could see the dragon had the moose in its claw and watched the dragon deal a deathblow to the spine.

Then, it was over. Othala relaxed and began tearing into the moose's belly, eating the organ meats and entrails. Kalena sat up and took a deep breath, releasing Romarin as he sat up too.

"Well, that was exhilarating," Romarin remarked wryly. "Are you all right?" He climbed down Othala's back and waited for her.

"I think so," Kalena said. "I feel pretty beaten up, though." She stood up and slowly slid from the dragon's back to the ground again. She hadn't had time to notice where they were. They were in a clearing on one of the cliffs, surrounded by pine trees as far as she could see. It was much colder here and there were several inches of snow on the ground. The trees were flocked as though it recently snowed. Kalena shivered and pulled her cloak around her. Without Othala's direct warmth, she quickly became chilled.

"We can't stay here long without a fire," he remarked. "Not without some food." He turned to Othala who had finished the organ meats and was now happily munching on the ribs. "Othala, can you spare some meat?"

The dragon looked up from the carcass, her face bloody from the meal. :*You don't have food?*

"Not much," he said. "And certainly no meat. The fireworms took everything when they attacked."

For a moment, it looked to Kalena as though Othala might refuse. : *How much?*

"Not much," Romarin assured her. "Not even a full haunch."

The dragon looked down at the moose and then bit into a haunch, tearing it from the carcass. She tossed the bloody mass at Romarin's feet. :*Give me what you do not use.*

"Thank you," Romarin said. He turned to Kalena. "Which do you want to do? Butcher the meat or gather wood for a fire?"

Kalena looked at the bloody mass in disgust. "Is there anything edible?"

He bent down and looked at the haunch, flipping it over. "I think so. We'll have to pull the skin away and clean it with snow."

She sighed. "I'll get the wood. It'll warm me up." She stomped her feet a bit to get the blood flowing in her toes again.

He nodded. "I'll clean up the meat."

The clearing ended uphill some fifty yards away. Kalena walked for several yards before faltering and gasping for breath. The rarified air took her by surprise. While Citadel Heights was in the foothills of the Shadow Mountains, it wasn't nearly as high as she now was. She was thirsty too and pulled her canteen and drank. She turned and looked back at Romarin and the dragon. Neither seemed to be paying attention to her, so she turned and walked uphill again, this time taking the pace slower and letting herself rest occasionally.

It took her longer to gather the firewood than she expected. Most of the deadfall was too big to carry, let alone snap with her hands, so he had to resort to looking for dead branches on live trees. The lack of air also made her work harder and she had to stop and rest frequently. Kalena wasn't used to this, being in peak condition as a *Chi'lan* warrior. By the time she returned with the bundle of wood, Romarin had skinned and dressed the meat, cutting them into manageable slabs. Othala was apparently sated from her meal and had curled herself up in a tight circle, like a cat taking a nap. The dragon's breath made her chest rise and fall rhythmically.

If Romarin was annoyed at the time it took her to gather wood, he didn't show it. "Good, that'll be enough for dinner. We'll have to gather more wood for tonight."

"Tonight?" she said surprised. She dropped the wood on the ground where Romarin and stomped out a firepit in the snow. "We're staying here?"

"Othala is tired," Romarin said, glancing at the dragon. "She didn't say much about it, but that was a fair amount of flying for a dragon her size to do."

"Her size?" Kalena mused. "She's enormous."

Romarin laughed. "She's small, actually. The big males grow to two hundred feet or more in length."

Kalena stared at the sleeping dragon. "I had no idea," she admitted. "She's the only dragon I've ever seen." She knelt down, rocking back on her heels to arrange the wood in a configuration for a fire, starting with a few larger pieces to shield the tinder from the snow and then the tinder, followed by some larger sticks. She pulled out her flint from a pouch she kept on her belt and struck her dagger against it, causing sparks near the tinder. It took a few tries but eventually, she had a fire started. Romarin pulled one of the sticks she had gathered and started whittling a point on each end. He skewered some of the meat and thrust the stick point first into the snow. It took a few attempts to get it to stand upright, but he eventually did and grinned.

"Not too bad," he said.

Kalena nodded. She knew she was cold mostly because she hardly had anything to eat. As the meat began to cook, Kalena felt her stomach rumble. It seemed to take longer than she would've liked but she waited patiently for Romarin to pull the meat off the skewer and hand some to her.

The meat was too hot to eat with bare hands, so she kept her gauntlets on, despite the smelly moose fat that rolled down her fingertips. Both she and Romarin ate for a while without talking while more meat cooked on the fire.

After the first skewer was gone, Kalena looked at Othala, who was still sleeping peacefully. "It's hard to believe that the fireworms are even related to dragons."

Romarin stopped in mid-bite and considered Othala. "There are similarities, to be sure."

"Didn't the dragons come from the *Fyr*?"

"Aye, they did," Romarin said. "But so did the worms."

"Rhyn'athel freed them too?"

Romarin shrugged. "I don't know."

Kalena retrieved another spit from the fire and pulled off the meat. "I am so hungry," she confessed. She pulled a few pieces of meat off the skewer and handed Romarin some.

He pulled some of the meat off the skewer and began eating it. "So, Kalena, why did you choose to become *Chi'lan*?"

Kalena paused. "Well, my family was *Chi'lan*. And the *Chi'lan* are all I've ever known."

"But you've lost so much," Romarin said. "Sorry," he said quickly, when he saw the hurt in her eyes.

"No, it's all right," she said softly. "I think I was destined to be *Chi'lan*, just as you were destined to be king."

"Just as you were destined to save my life," Romarin said.

Kalena snorted. "Without your magic, I would've been killed."

"And yet, you managed to save me," he said. "I owe you something."

Kalena looked up from her meat in surprise. He owed her something? She couldn't imagine what she could ask from him. The things she truly wanted were not his to give. "All right," she said. "Tell me a story."

Romarin blinked. "A story?"

"Yes, Cahal must have told you many wonderful stories," Kalena said. "He seemed to be an endless source of them after we finished training."

Romarin grinned. "He used to tell me stories when I was a *chi'li'a*. Even when I was a young *Chi'lan*, he'd still sit and reminisce about the old days." He paused. "What would you like to hear?"

"Pick one," she said. "One I haven't heard of."

"Well, with Cahal, that might be very difficult. He did go on about the olden days. Have you heard any stories about Tamar?"

"I heard Rhyn'athel bested Tamar and they became great friends after that."

"Aye, they did," Romarin said. "But did you know that he fell hopelessly in love with a woman named Jera?"

Kalena finished her meat and shook her head. "I've never heard the story."

"Ah, then you are missing out on quite a story," Romarin said. "Let me begin."

Kalena rested against the packs as Romarin began to tell the story. His eyes glowed red in the firelight as he told it. He had a fine voice, she decided, and he was very handsome. She hadn't lied to him about that. He had inherited his looks from the warrior god.

"Tamar was one of Queen Lachlei's greatest *Chi'lan*," Romarin said. "Cahal was young then – very young, having just made *Chi'lan* before Lachlei's husband died at the hands of the death god. Tamar was large even for a *Lochvaur* – many said he even had some Ansgar blood in him, because he was so large and muscular. But Tamar was pureblood.

So tough was Tamar that he survived the *Athel'cen* wars alongside Cahal. When Lachlan and my ancestor, Elsonre, were born, he was chosen to be their guardian along with Cahal. And yet, his memory has faded into near obscurity, which is a shame."

"What happened?" Kalena asked, intrigued.

"Eventually, they became your ancestors," Romarin said. "But I'd wager no one has told you the remarkable story."

"I'd like to hear it."

Chapter Thirty-One

Romarin leaned back. "I'll try to remember the story as Cahal told it, but you'll have to forgive me if I don't remember everything. It was fall, right around the time of Lachlan and Elsonre Ah'rhyn's births. Snow had begun falling in the Lochvaren Mountains. Cahal and Tamar rode side-by-side as they slowly made their way down the King's Highway towards Caer Lochvaren. Although it was barely autumn, the snows had come early this year in the mountains and Tamar didn't like the ominous clouds."

"The King's Highway?" Kalena repeated. "That's far north of Citadel Heights."

Romarin nodded. "The road and the land belong to Allarun now. But at that time, it was *Lochvaur* domain. They were riding downhill through conifers and pines. It wasn't a big road, despite the grand name – it barely had enough room for two men to ride together.

"Tamar was a big man, even for a *Lochvaur*. Despite being pureblood, some had questioned whether he was *Shara'kai*. Rhyn had never remarked about Tamar's bloodline, but the god considered his *Chi'lan* equals, regardless of being first-blood or not.

"Both Tamar and Cahal were good friends – and were friends with Rhyn'athel, who had chosen to stay for a while with his people. He had to undo the damage caused by Areyn when the death god led his army of demons and undead against them. They wanted to return home quickly, for they both knew that mead would be waiting for them."

Kalena laughed. "*Chi'lan* never change."

Romarin grinned. "No, they don't." He paused and continued. "The two warriors rode in silence for a while. The clouds overhead grew darker and a gloom settled on the land.

"'I wish we were further along,' Tamar grumbled. Already a few inches of snow had fallen, making the way more treacherous for their horses.

Cahal looked up into the sky. The thick snow now swirled around them. 'I don't know,' he said. 'We may have to seek someplace to weather the storm.'

'I don't think there's a single structure until we get to the plains,' Tamar said. 'They say these mountains are haunted by spirits.'

"Cahal chuckled.

"'What?' Tamar said sharply. 'You don't believe in spirits – not after all we've been through?'

"'No spirits of mortal men haunt these mountains," Cahal assured him. 'The dead go to Areyn's or Rhyn'athel's realm, depending on which god they serve.'

"'But there are other spirits," Tamar insisted. 'The mountains have magical creatures that live throughout. Faeries, woodland sprites, spirits that inhabit both forest and glen...'

"Cahal shook his head and chuckled. 'Tamar, Tamar, we've never seen these spirits.'

"Tamar met Cahal's gaze. 'Just because you haven't seen them, Cahal, doesn't mean they don't exist.'"

"And do they?" Kalena asked.

Romarin shook his head. "I don't know. Cahal was, by his very nature, a skeptic, even though he had seen magic from gods and first-bloods. He had fought and killed demons and undead, but until he actually saw something or felt magic, he was unwilling to accept simple bogie tales."

"I can see that," Kalena said. "Even though Cahal never discussed spirits." She chuckled. "I wonder what he thinks about the dreams he's been sending me."

Romarin nodded. "Cahal and Tamar entered a forest of lodge pole pines. At that moment, they heard a shriek of terror. Both men jumped, drawing their swords. Their horses neighed and tossed their heads as another scream for help came through the forest. Cahal reined his horse sharply, but Tamar had already turned his horse and spurred it into the woods.

"Cahal shouted after him, but if the other *Chi'lan* had heard him, he didn't acknowledge it. The snow wasn't very deep, but the footing was treacherous and Cahal was afraid that Tamar's horse would founder with the big man on it. Cursing, Cahal followed him.

"Cahal's horse plowed through the snow, but his roan was nowhere near the size of Tamar's bay and slowed as it hit the drifts. Tamar had a lead on Cahal too, and soon the big warrior was out of sight as he crested a hill. Amid the frightened wails came another noise that caused Cahal to grind his teeth. The soft howls of wolves echoed through the forest.

"As he crested the rise, the sounds of battle reached his ears. Below him in the ravine, Tamar was fighting white ghostly wolves with red eyes and blood that dripped from their tongues and five-inch saber teeth. *Yeth Hounds*. The demon hounds of Areyn Sehduk."

"Yeth Hounds?" Kalena repeated. "But they were supposed to be gone after Areyn left."

"That's what Cahal thought too," Romarin said. "But Cahal had seen plenty of Yeth to know those demon wolves on sight.

"Tamar had ridden into the pack of demon wolves and was slashing at the creatures in an effort to reach the lone figure huddled against one of the small pines.

"Cahal knew from his own experiences and from Lachlei's accounts that the creatures could only be killed through magic or adamantine, and that Tamar had ridden to his death, since he only had an adamantine sword – and no magic. Cahal spurred his horse towards the snapping demons and swung his adamantine sword.

"The first Yeth to attack lunged at his roan and slashed into the gelding. Cahal slammed his sword into the wolf as his horse screamed and reared. Somehow, he managed to keep his seat and his sword's blade shuddered as it cut deep into the wolf. The wolf faded and disappeared and Cahal found himself slicing air. Another wolf attacked and his roan responded, slamming its hooves into the creature, its adamantine-alloyed horseshoes stomped into the wolf's head. Trampled, the wolf screamed in pain before disappearing.

"Cahal reined his horse and saw Tamar cutting into another Yeth Hound and turning towards the woman. She was a *Lochvaur*, but from where, Cahal didn't know. She wore nothing special – breeches, shirt, cloak and boots of brown, stained with her blood. Her red-gold tresses were plastered to her face and she was slumped against the tree in an odd angle. The only part of her skin that was exposed had a deep gash from the wolves' teeth. Another gash ran along her arm. Cahal could see she had tried to trace runes in the snow with her blood at cardinal points in a circle. The circle was maybe fifteen feet around her. The wards, if they existed at all, were drawn in a great hurry.

"Another Yeth leapt at Cahal and he slammed his pommel into the creature. The force of his blow threw the wolf towards the circle and the wolf screamed and disappeared as it touched the circle. That gave Cahal an idea. 'Tamar!' Cahal shouted. 'Get into the circle!'

"Tamar needed no further urging and they both crossed the ward runes. There was just enough room for both horses and not much more. To Cahal's amazement, the Yeth Hounds hung back."

"Was she a first-blood?" Kalena asked. She hadn't heard of any ancestor of hers being first-blood.

"Patience," Romarin chuckled. "I'm getting to that."

Kalena sat back and listened.

"Tamar checked the woman, who was not much more than a girl. I think she was a little younger than you are. He marveled that she was still alive. Meantime, Cahal kept his eyes on the demons. He didn't trust the wards to hold, but at the same time, he knew that the ward circle was perhaps their only shield. A Yeth Hound came closer, but the moment it touched the circle, it shied back with a yelp.

"Cahal recognized the wards' power as being cast by more than a simple witch. He knew the woman was a sorceress, if not a first-blood. Tamar bandaged her while Cahal kept eye on the demons, wondering what the woman could've done that would've brought on the hounds of Areyn's wrath."

Kalena had closed her eyes as she listened to the story. Now, she opened them. "I thought only first-bloods could do magic."

"That's usually the case, but not always," Romarin said. "It's unusual, but not rare for those without god's blood, except maybe in their very distant past, to be able to cast spells and perform magic, but it happens. Sometimes the magic is different than that of a first-blood's."

"There are types of magic?"

"Oh yes." Romarin grinned. "Most *Eleion* magic stems from having a god, either *Laeca* or *Athel'cen* in their lineage, but not always. Some *Eleion* practice a type of magic, often referred to as 'witch-magic.' It relies on certain substances and elements to complete the spells. I've heard of *Shara'kai* and even *Ansgar* being able to use that magic."

Kalena stared into the fire. "Can anyone practice it?"

Romarin shrugged. "I really don't know. At one time, all *Eleion* used mindspeak and simple charms and wards were common." He paused. "Do you want me to continue?"

"Yes, please."

"The woman, named Jera awoke in terror as Tamar was bandaging her. She was very young – not even twenty. She was very pretty but the wounds were grievous, and they would scar terribly. But that made little difference to Tamar. He was instantly drawn to Jera.

"After their introductions, Jera told them she was from North Marches. She was trying to escape the Yeth Hounds by coming to Caer Lochvaren.

"'North Marches? It's been destroyed for almost a year.' Cahal stared at her.

"Jera began weeping. Tamar glared at Cahal.

"'I know, I was there. The demon was there,' Jera said.

"'Why are the Yeth pursuing you?' Tamar asked.

"'Because I am marked,' she whispered, her voice was hollow. 'Because I should've died in North Marches.' She shivered violently.

"'That's nonsense,' Tamar said softly. He pulled his cloak from his shoulders and wrapped her in it.

"'Thank you,' she said. 'But you too will be the Yeth's victims if you stay. You see, Areyn Sehduk, the death god, marked those from North Marches for death. I am cursed. The Yeth have chased me all this time.'

"As Tamar continued to try to bandage her face, Jera grasped his hand and laid it flat against her cheek. Cahal watched in amazement at his friend's hand began to glow. Beneath his hand, Jera's wound closed and healed. 'You're a healer,' Cahal gasped. 'Are you first-blood?'

"Jera shook her head. 'No,' she said, as she took Tamar's hand and pressed it against her other wounds.

"Daylight shifted into twilight and the demon wolves waited outside the circle, trying to spook their horses or press the men into running. Cahal tied his horse to the tree and cut what boughs he could to make a fire. They sat around the fire, hoping the demon wolves would leave, but each time Cahal thought the Yeth had left, he spied glowing eyes just outside the firelight.

"Jera told the men her story. She had been wounded in the battle, but as she was not *Chi'lan*, she had managed to escape the slaughter, mostly due to luck. 'Only that I haven't truly escaped,' she said ruefully. 'The Yeth pursue me.'

"'For a whole year?' Cahal asked dubiously.

"Jera shook her head. 'I managed to trick them several times with magic. And my ward runes aren't too bad.'

"Cahal glanced at the circle, still visible in the firelight. 'I'd say they weren't bad at all.'

"Tamar held her gently to keep her warm, and Cahal noted that the big warrior was caressing her hair. 'No, they're not.'

"Cahal and Tamar discussed their situation in mindspeak, so they would not frighten Jera. For even though she was very tough to evade the Yeth for so long, both men could see she was exhausted and at her limit. They knew they had one chance – and that was to make it to Caer Lochvaren. They knew the god of warriors could destroy the Yeth with a single thought and break the curse – but the city was a day away.

"That night, Cahal and Tamar took turns at the watch. It was Cahal's turn when dawn came, and with it, the Yeth Hounds had disappeared. Tamar had wrapped his cloak and blankets around himself and Jera. It was obvious the big warrior had been taken with her, but Cahal wondered if that was wise. Yeth Hounds were relentless in their pursuit of their prey and while Jera would be safe within the walls of Caer Lochvaren, he doubted any of them would make it that far if the Yeth pursued. Still, Cahal knew they couldn't leave Jera to her fate, and even if they did, there was no guarantee the Yeth Hounds wouldn't hunt the two *Chi'lan* once they had finished off Jera.

"Tamar opened his eyes and shifted a bit. The ground was cold, despite their blankets and the fire, and it had been a worrisome and uncomfortable night for all. Still, Jera had slept soundly in Tamar's arms; she trusted her two protectors with her life. Cahal marveled at Jera's ability to stay alive for so long. She probably had sought refuge in whatever towns she could find along the way – the Yeth couldn't pass thresholds or enter gates, but they could maraud the countryside until the townspeople forced her out.

"Beyond his ability to mindspeak, Cahal had no other magic, but he had been around first-bloods and Rhyn'athel long enough to sense the talent. Jera was at least a sorceress. Maybe not as powerful as Lachlei, but she was powerful enough. Her ability to heal herself and draw ward runes made her as powerful as most first-bloods. She had survived this long because of her powers.

"Perhaps she could help them survive.

"'Tamar, it's time,' Cahal said.

"'The Yeth are gone?' Tamar asked.

"'Ask Jera, I think she'd know.' Cahal looked at Jera as she slept.

"Tamar looked down at her. 'Jera,' he said, shaking her gently. Jera's eyes opened. 'Cahal thinks you'd know if the Yeth are gone.'

"Jera rubbed her eyes. There were large and pale silver, almost luminescent. She looked up at Tamar, her gaze full of trust. 'They'll be back soon,' she said. 'They have sought out other prey nearby.'

"They rode out of the protective circle and towards the King's Highway once more. Jera had healed the horses as well as any cuts both men sustained. She sat behind Tamar; she was so small and light, she was no burden to the big warhorse. They rode towards Caer Lochvaren, alert and ready for the Yeth, but none of the wolves came.

"After four hours of vigilant riding, Cahal began to wonder if the Yeth had given up their quarry. After all, they were in *Lochvaur* lands and Rhyn'athel still lived in Caer Lochvaren. But just as he began to think they were free, they heard a loud howl of a wolf that was nearly on top of them.

"Tamar reined his horse sharply, drawing his sword, and Cahal did likewise.

"'No!' said Jera. 'They're far away. Their voices grow more distant to trick you into running towards them.'

"Cahal nodded. He remembered hearing of Lachlei's encounter with the demon wolves. Cahal clapped his legs to his horse's sides and Tamar did likewise and they rode towards Caer Lochvaren at a gallop.

"The howling grew louder, fueling both horses' urgency to gallop, but even as the *Chi'lan* pulled away, the howling slowly grew dimmer. Cahal fought the urge to think they were escaping. The dimming howls suggested that the pack was approaching – but were he and Tamar still running away from Yeth or were the Yeth lying in ambush somewhere along the road? He couldn't guess.

"He looked at Tamar, whose face was grim. Jera had hidden her face in his cloak and he could see she was frightened. 'Where are they?' he shouted.

"Jera looked up. Her eyes were wide and red-rimmed, and she shook her head. 'I don't know!'

"The howls grew dim. The horses frothed and increased speed. Cahal glanced behind and at that moment, saw movement behind them among the trees. They were perfectly camouflaged against the snow save for their red, glowing eyes and maws that dripped blood. The Yeth were twenty lengths back. Cahal knew the Yeth would gain on them within a few scant minutes.

"'Tamar!' Cahal shouted.

"*I can help*, Jera's voice came clear to both their minds. *If Tamar will fight. Stay back, Cahal, for I can't touch you...*

"*I won't leave Tamar*, Cahal said.

"*Get Rhyn*, Tamar said. *The Yeth should not be in this world.*

"With that, Tamar reined his horse. The horse began to slow and Cahal cursed as he saw Tamar turn the horse to face the Yeth. Cahal reined his own steed to bring it around for a fight. To his surprise, he saw Jera upright behind the cantle, her hands gesturing in a way he had never seen before. Blue fire issued from her fingertips and enveloped the horse, Tamar and her. With a yell, Tamar turned and charged the oncoming demon wolves.

"*Go!* Tamar shouted mentally. Three of the Yeth attacked, but the moment they touched the glowing fire, they screamed and disintegrated. Tamar swung his sword, slicing into the beasts as they tried to find a way beyond Jera's defenses.

"A Yeth spotted Cahal and charged towards him. Cahal needed no more urging and turned the roan towards Caer Lochvaren. He rode as quickly as he dared and within an hour, arrived at the gates.

"To his surprise, the warrior god met him as he dismounted. 'Cahal,' Rhyn'athel said. 'Where is Tamar?'

"Cahal lowered his head and shook it. 'The Yeth.' He felt Rhyn'athel's mental touch and opened his mind to the god.

"Rhyn'athel's face became grim. 'Come with me.'

"At that, Cahal felt a sickening lurch in his stomach and he stood beside Rhyn'athel, sword drawn. The god had his own Sword of Power, *Teiwaz*, drawn. He had transported both of them to the place where Tamar and Jera had made their stand.

"And yet, the Yeth were gone. Tamar's horse stood close by, frothing and sweaty, shaking from exhaustion. Nearby, Tamar sat, Jera lay against him, both wounded and covered with blood.

"Tamar saw Rhyn'athel and Cahal, and grinned. 'She held them off as long as she could,' he said. 'There must have been a hundred of them.' He stroked her blood-encrusted hair.

"Rhyn'athel knelt down and touched Jera. 'A survivor of North Marches.' With that, Jera's wounds closed and her eyes fluttered open as Rhyn'athel touched Tamar and healed him as well.

"'The warrior god,' Jera whispered. 'The rumors I heard were true.' She bowed her head.

"Rhyn'athel shook his head. 'Don't, my child,' he said. 'You've been far braver than anyone would've been.'

"'Please, Rhyn, lift the curse from her,' Tamar asked. He stood up slowly and unsteadily and he helped Jera to her feet.

"'There is no need,' Rhyn'athel said. 'You have lifted the curse yourselves. Areyn left the Yeth in this world to hunt down any survivors. Once a Yeth was killed, it could not return. You have destroyed the last of that evil.'

"You see, the Yeth were gone, once they died and left this world. They could not return until they were summoned again," Romarin said. "But that didn't happen until Allarun. What could not be stopped by magic or by force could only be defeated when Tamar and Jera combined their abilities. That is why they defeated the demons."

Chapter Thirty-Two

Romarin's voice had change tenor as he told the story of Tamar and Jera. It was deeper, softer and more rhythmic, almost magical in tone and quality. Kalena closed her eyes, letting his voice carry her far from this world and into the world that Cahal knew over a thousand years before. She had wrapped her cloak around her, and despite the cold air, she was very warm. The fire crackled close by, radiating its heat over her. Before Kalena knew it, she drifted asleep.

At some point, Romarin's words merged with her dreams, only he was Tamar, and she Jera. And yet, the dream felt wrong, and soon, she found herself riding beside a man who looked remarkably like Romarin.

Kalena looked around. She was leading an army beside the king. Frost hung in the air from her breath and she looked at the pine and conifers flocked with snow. The birch and aspen trees had long ago shed their leaves; their stark, white skeletons stretched upward towards a cerulean blue sky.

"It won't be long before we catch Silvain," the man said beside her. He grinned. "Elsonre will be bringing the rest of the Chi'lan up from Caer Lachlanel..." He paused as he studied her face. "What's wrong, beloved?"

Kalena shook her head. "I don't know." Her hand went instinctively to her belly and as she touched it, to her shock, she discovered she was pregnant.

The man looked concerned. "Cara, are you all right?"

Kalena felt a tremble in her gut. Was it the baby or nausea? She couldn't tell. "I'm fine, Lachlan, really, I am..."

Kalena awoke to someone shaking her gently. As her eyes fluttered open, she was greeted by blinding sunlight. The sky overhead was blue, but wispy cirrus clouds stretched across it. Romarin was kneeling down beside her. She blinked several times. As she did, she stared at Romarin's face. So much like Lachlan's, could he really be Lachlan's reincarnation?

"Are you all right?" Romarin asked. "You slept so deeply, I could barely wake you." He stood up and turned to tend to the fire. It was not much more than embers, and Kalena was now cold, despite the cloak.

Kalena blinked again. It was midmorning, by the look of the sun's position in the sky. She wondered how she slept so long. Perhaps she had been more tired than she realized.

Or, perhaps it had been the dream. The dream was fading even now. "I'm fine," she said with a slight smile. "You're quite a storyteller. I was dreaming about Tamar and Jera for quite a while." She hesitated. "I dreamt of Lachlan, too." She shivered in the cold.

"Really?" Romarin asked. His voice was even, which suggested to her that though he sounded nonchalant, he was curious.

Kalena rose and slowly stretched her cold-stiffened muscles. "I don't really remember much," she said. "Something you said must have made me dream about him last night."

"What did he look like?" Romarin pulled out the moose meat from a pile of snow he had made to store it. He spitted the pieces on sticks.

"Like you," she said. She smiled and he laughed.

"I would imagine so," Romarin said. "Rhyn'athel's sons tend to favor him, so it would be no surprise that I looked quite a bit like Lachlan."

"Do you think you're Lachlan?" As soon as the words left her mouth, she regretted it. Something in his eyes flickered with uncertainty.

"I don't know," he said. He turned away.

Kalena frowned and looked away, noticing for the first time that the dragon was gone. "Where's Othala?" she asked in alarm.

Romarin chuckled and the tension eased. "She's out hunting again. She told me that after she's eaten, she'll bring us to the fireworm lairs by tonight."

"She's been very helpful," Kalena remarked.

"She has," Romarin agreed.

Kalena sat next to him beside the fire and rubbed her cold hands. "I'll be glad when we're off this mountain and in fireworm territory."

"I won't be," Romarin remarked. "It'll still be very cold there, and we won't have Othala around to protect us. I don't know what would happen if several large fireworms attacked."

"Fireworms wouldn't dare attack a dragon, would they?"

Romarin nodded. "They would. Fireworms are quarrelsome beasts and not particularly fond of dragons. Othala didn't say much about it, but I suspect she's eating so she has enough reserve to fight them, if need be."

Kalena frowned as she stared into the fire. "I don't want Othala hurt."

"Nor do I," Romarin said, turning one of the spits. "Othala isn't fond of fireworms and they've been as much a threat to her as they've been to us." He turned the spit again. "Here, the meat is ready."

Kalena pulled a knife from her belt and stabbed the piece, dragging it off the spit. She was careful to not have the meat drop and carefully tasted it. The meat was tough and a bit fatty, but she was so hungry, she would've eaten it burnt.

They ate in silence and Kalena's mind wandered back to the dream. It had resonated with her somehow, and she wondered if what she was looking at was in the past – or the future. As she ate, she took furtive glances at Romarin and tried to match his face with that of what she could recall of Lachlan's. Were they the same? She didn't know. The dream had faded in her memory to the point where she couldn't be sure of anything.

The wind changed directions and the air grew colder. Romarin stood up and frowned, looking at the sky. The small bands of wispy cirrus were being overtaken by thicker, darker cumulus clouds. "What's wrong?" Kalena asked.

"The wind is from the east," Romarin remarked. "I don't like it."

"A storm?"

Romarin nodded once and continued scanning the skies. Kalena felt uneasy, more because of Romarin's reaction than anything she sensed on her own part. She had no magic, so sensing anything Romarin did was impossible. Still, she ate the meat swiftly.

"There!" Romarin said. "Get your bow."

Kalena followed his line of sight towards the darkening clouds. She could just make out one large dark form surrounded by several smaller ones. The dark form twisted and turned erratically, reminding Kalena of a hawk being chased by a group of smaller birds. "What is it?"

"It's Othala," Romarin said grimly. "And fireworms are attacking her."

Chapter Thirty-Three

Kalena scooped up her bow from on the ground next to the blankets. She hastily strung the bow and nocked an arrow, never letting her eyes leave the macabre dance in the skies. Othala was flying hard, twisting and turning to keep herself away from the fireworms, but both she and the fireworms were out of Kalena's bowshot. Even if they did get comfortably within her range, Kalena wasn't sure if she could hit one of the fireworms without accidentally hitting Othala.

Kalena chanced a quick glance at Romarin. The king seemed focused on Othala and Kalena wondered if perhaps he was trying to guide Othala towards them. Kalena sensed Romarin's mindspeak, but could not hear it, as it was directed at the dragon.

"I'd feel more comfortable if she was below one hundred yards," Kalena said, taking aim even though the dragon and fireworms were over a thousand yards away. She tried following the erratic movements, but to little avail.

Romarin didn't even glance at her. "Can you hit a mark in three hundred?"

"Aye, but not one so erratic." Kalena pulled ten arrows from the quiver and stuck them in the snow point down. There were three fireworms and Othala.

"You'll have no choice," Romarin said. "You'll have to hit a soft area – mouth, eye or wings. Can you do it?"

Kalena chewed her lip. She had no choice. Othala was counting on it. "Yes."

"Wait for my signal and be ready. We won't have much time."

Kalena nodded, wondering what he meant. Maybe Romarin knew something she didn't? She felt her shoulders tense as she chose and tracked the largest of the three fireworms. Despite the cold, sweat tricked down her forehead into her eyes and she blinked and shook her head several times. Her bow fingers were numb even though she wore gauntlets and she could feel the tension in every part of her body. Still, she forced herself to focus on the fireworm.

The dragon and fireworms drew closer. Kalena couldn't be sure, but they looked like they were less than five hundred yards away. She wasn't sure because without reference points other than Othala's size, she could only hazard a guess. Othala dwarfed the fireworms who snapped and tried to latch themselves onto her. In horror, Kalena realized that was what the worms were doing.

The largest fireworm snapped at Othala's head, keeping the dragon's attention. Othala had ripped into the large fireworm's skin – Kalena could see the dark blood ooze from gouges where Othala had lashed out with her claws. At the same time, the other two fireworms leapt at her. One fireworm latched on Othala's spiny back and tried to coil itself around the dragon's body. The sharp fireworm claws flailed upwards, trying to rip Othala's thin wing membranes.

"Now!" Romarin shouted.

Kalena hesitated. They were still not within three hundred yards, much less one hundred. She had been following the large fireworm, but that wasn't the real danger. She shifted her aim to the fireworm along Othala's back, hoping to miss the big dragon and hit the fireworm's eye. She let loose the arrow.

At the last second, Othala and the fireworm rolled and the arrow hit the dragon along the side, snapping the arrow. Kalena sucked in a breath in horror, half expecting the dragon to plummet out of the sky, but instead Othala simply roared and snapped at the fireworm along her back. The larger fireworm slashed at her face, forcing her to turn to face it again.

"Fire!" Romarin ordered.

Kalena pulled an arrow from the snow and nocked it, her hands trembling. *What if she hit Othala in a vital spot?* She aimed again, this time at the larger fireworm. Maybe Othala could get the one entangling her if she had one less adversary. Kalena aimed and fired.

The arrow sailed true towards the intended target. It caught the fireworm's thin membrane between the fifth finger and arm bones, punching a hole right through it and lodging into the second arm bone. The fireworm shrieked and plummeted to the ground, unable to fly. Romarin drew his sword and ran forward, hoping to catch the beast before it could attack them.

Kalena was about to follow him when she heard Romarin's voice in her head. :*Keep shooting.*

Kalena pulled and nocked an arrow just in time to see the third fire-worm charge right towards her, breathing fire. Kalena gasped and ran, barely escaping the flames of the angry creature as it came at her. The rarified air burned in her lungs as she tried to scramble towards the forest, away from the rocky outcropping.

She sensed, rather than saw, the flames as the fireworm attacked. At the last second, she dodged and twisted, shooting the arrow at the creature's eye. Kalena expected the arrow to glance off the tough hide, but to her complete astonishment, the arrow hit high, just below the thin orbital ridge and penetrated. The arrow buried itself through bone and into brain. With a desperate slash, the fireworm tried to rip the shaft from its head as at plummeted to the ground. Kalena drew her sword and between the thrashing death throws, hacked the creature's head off.

Chapter Thirty-Four

Then, it was silent. Kalena stood for a moment staring at the dead creature, the widening circle of blood, and at herself. Blood coated her gauntlets and arms, and she felt sick. She swayed for a moment before collapsing, throwing up what little breakfast she had. She continued to retch even after her food had come up, until she felt a strong hand on her shoulder.

She looked up. Romarin was kneeling beside her. "Are you all right?"

She shook her head. "I'm sorry..."

"Don't be," Romarin said. "Let me help you stand up." His gauntleted hand slipped under her arm and he helped her to her feet. He held her for a moment longer even after she was steady on her feet again. She looked into his eyes.

So like Lachlan's, she thought. She pushed those thoughts aside and looked around for the dragon. She was nowhere to be seen. "Where's Othala?"

"When you shot the first fireworm, Othala was able to kill the one on her back. She's gone to clean her wounds. She'll be back soon." Romarin looked at her. "Cahal was right – you're quite a warrior. I don't think I could've made that shot." He pointed to the dead fireworm beside them.

"Luck," Kalena said. She stared down at the fireworm's glassy eyes. "I don't think I could've done that again in a thousand years." She bent down and picked up the sword and followed her steps in the snow to retrieve her bow. Taking what little clean snow she could find, she wiped both weapons clean of blood and dried them on her cloak.

"That's some luck," Romarin said. "Let's get back to our camp and get ready. I have a feeling that once Othala gets back, she's going to want to leave this place as quickly as possible."

Kalena nodded and followed him back. Their campfire was smoldering now and the meat was burnt, but Kalena had no appetite. She picked up the few blankets and items they had left and bundled them up as tightly as she could. Just as she was about to sit down, Romarin held a cup of hot tea out to her.

"What's this?" She eyed it dubiously. It smelled like one of Daimhan's concoctions.

"It'll settle your stomach," Romarin said. "And help keep you warm. You'll need to have something to eat before Othala gets back."

Kalena drank the tea slowly. It tasted faintly of ginger and some other spices she didn't recognize, but as promised, it seemed to make her feel better. She sat back down at the fire and grimaced. "I hate killing."

To her surprise, Romarin laughed. But when she looked at him, there was little mirth in his expression. "So do I," he said. "Which makes us odd, I suppose. Warriors who hate war. It seems so contradictory."

"And yet, isn't Rhyn'athel the god of both life and warriors?"

Romarin nodded. "He is. But he is not the god of war. War is the death god's domain. It always has been."

Kalena glanced over at the dead fireworm. "Somehow, we must find a way to stop this. The fireworms can't want this any more than we do."

"Assuming they're intelligent enough to understand," Romarin said. "Othala doesn't think so, but she isn't fond of them either."

Kalena nodded and looked into the sky. She spotted something dark rise from the lands to the north. Instinctively, she raised her bow and nocked an arrow.

"It's Othala," Romarin said.

Kalena lowered her bow and blinked as she watched the dragon circle once overhead before landing carefully. :*Son of Rhyn'athel, it is time to go.*

Kalena gasped as she saw the frightful rakes along the dragon's body. The gouges looked deep and while the bleeding appeared to have stopped, Kalena guessed that the dragon would have some terrible scars. "Is she ok?"

Othala turned her red eyes to Kalena. :*I am alive, thanks to you, Chi'lan. It is not often a Fyr-dragon owes a life-debt.*

"Will you be all right?"

The dragon grinned, showing her many teeth. :*The wounds are minor. Dragons are indeed tougher than men.*

Kalena returned the arrow to the quiver and unstrung the bow. Romarin mounted first, taking the packs and gently tying them to the dragon's spines in front. Kalena climbed up, careful not to touch the injured flesh. No matter how bold Othala sounded, Kalena guessed the wounds hurt. She pulled herself behind Romarin again.

Othala leapt into the sky and Kalena hung on, feeling her empty stomach lurch as the dragon became airborne. She closed her eyes against the rushing wind and the dizzying view below her. The air was cold, despite Othala's warmth and Kalena shivered involuntarily. When Kalena opened her eyes again, she could just make out the dark cliffs looming on the horizon.

"Is that where we're going?" she shouted above the wind.

:*Use mindspeak*, Romarin said. :*But yes, we're going there.*

Kalena frowned and stared at the cliffs. They looked ominous to her – a sharp knife-edge rising among the surrounding mountains. :*How are we going to approach them without being seen?* It took all her concentration to use mindspeak.

:*I will fly low*, said Othala. :*But I can't bring you right to the cliffs or I will be attacked.*

:*Is there any way for us to climb up them?* Romarin asked dubiously. :*They look too steep for us.*

:*The cliffs level behind them, and there is a knife-edge that runs from a nearby mountain to the top of the lairs*, Othala said. :*I'll be taking you just below the knife-edge – it will be the safest approach, and also the easiest for you to climb. But there are other dangers there – snow leopards and other wild animals that will kill a man.*

Kalena frowned. She didn't like the sound of this, but she'd rather take her chances with other animals than fireworms. As they flew, the sun began to dip towards the horizon and the air grew colder yet. Kalena said nothing, but found her mind getting sluggish in the cold wind. Her fingers felt numb and each movement felt like needle pricks. She couldn't feel her toes at all.

It was around sunset when Othala descended into the valleys below. Despite the dragon's size, the ride became unpleasant as the dragon began to fight the more turbulent wind closer to the peaks. Othala's wings beat harder and her tail now swung side to side in a rudder-like fashion to compensate for the wind. At one point in the valley, she turned left and followed up a valley west of the dark cliffs.

:*The turbulence is always bad here*, Othala said. :*I hate flying this low, but the fireworms are less likely to see us.*

Kalena felt sick. The jostling had made her already queasy stomach downright ill. She hoped she wouldn't vomit again, partially because it was embarrassing, but more because Romarin was in front of her. But she knew she had nothing left in her stomach to throw up, so she bit her lip and hung on. As she worked towards keeping the bile down, she stared at the massive stone cliffs. As she did so, she saw two forms detach from the cliffs and hurdle towards them at frightening speeds.

:*We've got company*, she announced.

Chapter Thirty-Five

Othala snarled something that reverberated through Kalena in what the *Chi'lan* guessed was the dragon's form of a curse. It wouldn't be long before the fireworms attacked Othala again. This low in the valley, Kalena could see the trees rush by and the animals scurry away as the dragon soared over them. It was warmer here, though not by much, because it was nearly winter and Kalena's feet were hurting with sharp needle-like pricks. Kalena could see that the dragon was having trouble keeping level at this altitude.

:*Can you outrun them?* Romarin asked as the dark shapes flew towards them at an alarming speed.

:*Not this low*, Othala said. :*If I were up higher and not battling the winds, I'd outrun them, but not here.*

:*If we go up, there's no way you'll get us close enough to the cliffs*, Romarin said. :*How far are we from the knife-edge?*

:*You're not thinking of having her land in that?* Kalena asked, glancing at the forests below.

:*Two days walk, maybe?* Othala shrugged. :*Make up your mind, son of Rhyn'athel. I must either leave you here now or take flight.*

Romarin glanced at Kalena. :*It's not that far.*

:*But we're in fireworm territory*, Kalena said. :*They'll come looking for us.*

:*A chance you'll have to take, Chi'lan, or give up on your quest*, Othala said. :*What is it, son of Rhyn'athel?*

:*Take us down*, Romarin said, but his mindspoken voice was grim. :*We won't have much time, so be prepared to run*, he told Kalena.

Kalena gave the mental equivalent of a nod. She didn't want to run, especially with her feet and hands hurting like they did, but the fireworms weren't giving any of them a choice. If they caught Othala this low, they might just kill the dragon, and Kalena and Romarin along with her. If Othala flew higher, she could get away, but the chance of getting back to the cliffs without the fireworms observing them would be impossible. This was their only chance.

:*Get ready*, Othala said, and at that moment, dove hard. Othala's attack on the moose was nothing compared to this dive – it was so steep and hard, that Kalena was sure Romarin would be impaled by a bony ridge spine through his chest. The dragon slammed hard, snapping and uprooting trees as she came to a thunderous stop.

:*Off! Off!* Romarin shouted in mindspeak, but Kalena didn't need the orders. She leapt from Othala's back, hit the ground and rolled. Her body slammed against broken branches, rocks and spongy dirt. She leapt to her feet, too keyed up to feel the pain and drew her sword.

Othala leapt into the air, her wings beating furiously, stirring up a maelstrom of dirt behind her. Kalena saw the dragon fly upwards as the fireworms approached. Othala twisted in mid-air and turn south towards her home. She was soon out of sight.

"Come on," Romarin said, "we have to leave now."

Kalena turned and saw Romarin with the packs. Silently, she took one of her packs and slung it over her shoulders before following him into the dark timber.

Kalena followed Romarin, amazed at his pace. He had to be just as stiff and sore as she was and yet, he seemed to have a reserve she'd seldom seen in other *Chi'lan*. He led her away from the clearing made by Othala and pressed northward towards the backside of the cliffs.

They had gone no more than a hundred yards when the fireworms screamed overhead. Instead of running, Romarin motioned Kalena to stop. Kalena took several slow, heavy breaths as she looked up, trying to get a glimpse of the twilight sky above the forest canopy.

:*Remain still*, Romarin said. :*In this dense timber, they'll be looking for movement.*

:*Yes*, Kalena replied, fighting the urge to nod. With the darkness would come some safety – at least from fireworms. She closed her eyes and forced herself to breathe more slowly. They would be safe under the cover of night.

With a final screech, the fireworms flew away. Romarin waited several minutes before giving Kalena the signal that they could move again. Kalena sagged and dropped to the ground, letting her sword fall beside her. She was so tired and hungry; she didn't care if a pack of fireworms attacked.

Romarin frowned and knelt beside her. "Are you all right?"

Kalena shook her head. "Just exhausted, I guess." She smiled weakly as Romarin pressed a canteen in her hands. Her hands trembled and the canteen slipped and fell into her lap. She stared at it dumbly.

Romarin scooped up the canteen, uncorked it and pressed the water to her lips. The water trickled in her parched mouth, but she was too exhausted to even swallow. She closed her eyes and fell into oblivion.

"Kalena! Kalena!" Romarin tried shaking her and slapping her awake, but she stayed unconscious. He cursed himself for not recognizing the signs that she was in trouble. She hadn't eaten except that morning – and what little she'd eaten she had thrown up. She had not drunk water once as far as he could tell and when he picked up her canteen; he found it was nearly full.

Kalena's energy was low. The fight and ride on the dragon had sapped the *Chi'lan*'s reserves. Without food, water and warmth, she would die.

Chapter Thirty-Six

Romarin pulled off the gauntlet on his good hand and touched Kalena's cheek. She was very cold and had no reserves left. He looked up into the night's sky again. She needed the warmth of a fire and needed it now, but the flames would attract the fireworms.

He shouldered their supplies and took her sword and sheathed it in her scabbard before picking her up. She wasn't a small woman and the years of *Chi'lan* training made her heavier with muscle than she looked, but she was far lighter than her brother's corpse had been. He winced at the thought. Would she too die on this failed expedition?

Romarin had seen many warriors die, both men and women, and yet, he knew Kalena's death would be the hardest for him to bear. She was pretty in a rough way, and even with Cahal's teasing attempts at playing matchmaker, Romarin knew he was falling for her.

:But I am her king and over twice her age, he thought.

He knew at some point, age wouldn't matter. Cahal had lived over fifteen hundred years, but he was more of an exception, rather than the rule. If Romarin and Kalena lived through the fireworm attacks, he wondered if their age differences would no longer be relevant. Without the fireworms, the only enemy would be Allarun – and Allarun was unlikely to attack anytime soon. Perhaps there would be a future for them both.

As he carried her deeper into the forest, away from Othala's landing place, he looked for anything that might provide shelter and might hide a small fire. Nothing availed itself readily and he carried her until he came to the leeward side of a hill. The snow was deep here, but he also knew it'd be less cold than the windward side. He pulled out the blankets, wrapped her in them and set her down gently.

He pressed his hand against her face and allowed his power to flow into her. "Stay with me, Kalena," he whispered as he felt her warm slightly. "Just a little while longer and we'll have shelter."

Romarin stomped and cleared as much of the snow as he could. He cut boughs off the trees nearby and laid the branches down for bedding. He then made a small lean-to with branches and boughs. He returned to Kalena and felt for a pulse. It was there, faint and cold, but she was still alive. He carried her to the lean-to and with some effort, dragged her inside atop the blanket and boughs, and then crawled in beside her.

She was very cold. Romarin knew he should probably have stripped them both of armor and clothing for maximum warmth, but that would take too long and he didn't dare chance leaving them both unprotected with fireworms so close. He took her cold hands in his and concentrated, allowing his power to flow into her. He didn't have much energy left, himself, but he was determined to not let her die. He took her close in his arms and kissed her cold face gently.

"Don't die, Kalena" he whispered. "Live for me." He turned his thoughts to his father, the great warrior god. :*Rhyn'athel, I beg you, save her.*

He looked down at Kalena, but could not be sure if the prayer had done anything. She looked as though she was just sleeping and her color seemed a little less gray. Exhaustion finally overtook him, and Romarin fell into a cold and uneasy sleep.

Kalena found herself standing in the fireworms' lair again. She stared at the bones that lay amid the gold and treasure. She felt a touch on her shoulder and turned to see Cahal standing beside her.

"I can feel you," she marveled. She gripped Cahal's arms in the traditional *Chi'lan* greeting and gave her old master a hug. "Why?"

"You're near death, Kally," Cahal said. "Romarin is doing what he can to keep you alive, but you must fight."

"I'm near death?" Kalena stared at Cahal. "What do you mean?"

Cahal smiled ruefully. "You let yourself be depleted – you know better as a *Chi'lan* you need to keep your strength up."

Kalena stared at him for a moment. "The cold? I'm going to die because of the cold?"

"*Chi'lan* have died for more trivial reasons. The fight with the fireworms taxed you. Romarin can't save you if you don't fight."

Kalena stared at Cahal. "What must I do?"

"You must want to live, Kally. Fight for consciousness."

"But I'm tired."

"You need to live. Romarin can't do this alone. You're his only chance at finding Torfar and putting an end to this curse."

She turned away and shook her head. "I had a dream about Lachlan and Cara."

"Did you?" Cahal's voice sounded neither surprised nor alarmed.

"You know, don't you?"

"There are certain things one learns in the Hall of the Gods."

"I'm Cara, aren't I?"

Cahal smiled enigmatically. "What do you think, Kally?"

"Is Romarin Lachlan's reincarnation?"

He shook his head. "I don't know, Kally."

"If he is..." She paused and looked into her mentor's eyes. "Cahal, what should I do?"

"You need to live," he said. "Go now before you die."

Kalena felt the painful tug of life and turned from him. She closed her eyes and forced herself back to consciousness.

Chapter Thirty-Seven

Daylight streamed into the lean-to when Kalena awoke. The warm sunlight made a patchwork quilt of light across her face and body. She was warm and comfortable – and very hungry and thirsty. The last thing she remembered was running, and feeling cold and exhausted. She moved and found she could not, and turned slowly to find herself in Romarin's arms.

She started in shock, but then hesitated. She *had* been cold – had she passed out last night? Her armor and clothing, as well as the lean-to, confirmed her suspicions. Romarin had brought her here and saved her life. He had used his own body heat to keep her warm.

Despite herself, she didn't find his proximity all that objectionable. He was handsome and he reminded her of her vision of Lachlan. But even as she considered him, she wondered if it was just a dream or a vision. Had she been Lachlan's consort in a previous life? Cahal seemed to think she was someone he had known.

Cahal. The name brought her around quickly. They were so close to finding him or what became of him. And they were so close to finding Torfar. She shifted in Romarin's arms and found him blinking awake. They were so close, their noses nearly touched. She saw Romarin's face flush a deep red and she laughed.

He removed his arms around her. "I'm sorry," he said. "I-I..."

"I was frozen," Kalena said, and by Romarin's relieved expression, she knew she guessed right. "Thank you. It was foolish of me to have not eaten anything after the fight." She smiled ruefully. "I forgot Cahal's basic tenets."

"Fighting requires energy," Romarin repeated from rote. "Energy comes from food. Without energy, you die."

Kalena chuckled. "Drilled that into you, too?"

Romarin nodded and grinned. "It's more important for first-bloods because of the magic."

Kalena became very serious. "I want to thank you for saving me." She leaned forward and kissed him on his lips.

His lips were cold, as hers were, and the touch was fleeting, if powerful. Despite the circumstances, she could almost see herself falling in love with him. Romarin's face turned red again and Kalena laughed. "Now, what would the other *Chi'lan* say about that?" he muttered.

"Well, you're the first man I've ever slept with – at least, the entire night," she said wryly, and seeing his expression, burst out laughing.

Romarin laughed too, and hugged her. "By Rhyn'athel's sword, I'm glad you're alive."

"By the gods, I'm famished," Kalena said, pulling herself from his warm embrace. She tried to sit at first, but the lean-to was very low. She managed a kind of kneeling squat that allowed her to pull the packs from the entrance and rummage inside them. She found one of the canteens and pulled it out. "And thirsty, too." She uncorked the canteen and found a good portion of the water had frozen. She drank what little there was and corked it again. "Do we have any food?"

"Not much," Romarin said, propping himself up on one elbow. "I'm afraid I had to use most of it to keep you alive."

Kalena nodded. Of course, he would've. She had seen him become exhausted when he healed others; he probably needed food to give her energy to keep her warm during the night. She dug in the packs and pulled out a few hard tack biscuits. "Is this it?"

Romarin nodded.

Despite her hunger, Kalena knew she had to share what was left. She split the hard tack between them. "Maybe we can hunt?"

"I don't know," Romarin said. "Would there be animals this close to the fireworms? The area around Othala was bereft of animals."

Kalena nodded. "And could we chance a fire to cook the meat? Certainly it would attract fireworms."

Romarin nodded grimly. "If we can find a shelter that would hide the flame – a cave or overhanging rock formation, I'd chance it, even at night. Othala gave me the impression that the path along the knife-edge is mostly ignored, so we might be able to risk a fire in the daylight."

Kalena nodded slowly. A small campfire might go unnoticed in the daytime, especially if they kept it from smoking much. Still, she wondered how good the fireworms' sense of smell was.

Less than an hour later, Kalena and Romarin began walking towards the backside of the cliffs they had seen the night before. Kalena had strung her bow, keeping it ready for both fireworms and for any game that might come across their path. The lodgepole pines ran thick here and threw both warriors in a pervasive twilight. It was quiet here too, save for the crunch of snow and pine needles.

Romarin had melted the water in their canteens with a single command, but food was elusive. By mid-day, Kalena began to wonder if pine needles might taste good. She was trudging along behind Romarin when the king stopped. She hesitated and followed his hand as it pointed towards something moving in the forest.

Chapter Thirty-Eight

Kalena could not believe their luck. On the other side of the ridge were several elk, their red fur glinting against the dark timber. The creatures were moving slowly; Kalena guessed that she and Romarin were upwind of them, otherwise, they would've fled. A small elk would be more than enough for them both, assuming they caught one.

:*Can you hit one at this distance?* Romarin asked.

Kalena frowned. It was just within three hundred yards – the limit she felt comfortable with a bow. Even if she did get a good shot in, there was still a matter of tracking the beast. The blood trail would no doubt bring predators to the kill. She wasn't worried about wolves, but Othala had mentioned snow leopards and other predators, which she couldn't be sure they could fend off. Then, there was the ever-present danger of fireworms...

She brought her bow up and nocked an arrow. She watched carefully as a young cow elk came through the dark timber. Whispering a quick prayer to Rhyn'athel, Kalena took aim and shot.

The arrow flew true and hit the cow elk in the chest. The elk leapt up and began running only to stumble and fall a few yards away. The other elk scattered at the cow elk's odd movements.

Romarin patted Kalena's shoulder. :*Nice shot*, he said in mindspeak, and they walked slowly towards the elk.

Kalena followed Romarin, nocking another arrow in case a predator might appear. When they arrived at the elk, it was obvious how well placed the shot was. The arrow had pierced the chest, going straight through the lungs and into the heart, killing the animal quickly. Together, they dressed and began butchering the animal with their knives.

"I hate having to risk a fire," Romarin said, as they finished up. "But we can't eat raw meat and raw meat won't pack as well."

Kalena nodded and cleaned the blood from her gauntlets. "We have some salt, so we might be able to preserve a bit," she said.

Within an hour, they had gathered wood and started a fire. Despite their attempts, the fire proved to be a bit smokier than either of them would've preferred, but both were so hungry, they began eating the meat half cooked from the spits. While Kalena ate, Romarin melted snow in cups and added herbs to them in a medicinal-tasting tea. Kalena didn't object when he handed her a cup.

"It'll help keep you warm," he said as he drank his own cup.

Kalena drank slowly, feeling the liquid warm her as she sipped. The tea seemed to make her joints feel less stiff and sore and she found herself relaxing a little. As she did, she stared up into the cerulean blue sky that peeked above the treetops.

Her mind wandered back to her dream with Cahal. Had she been so near death she could actually talk to him? And was Cahal really dead, or was this just a dream? She didn't hold much hope for finding Cahal alive, certainly not after all this time. But she did wonder if her dreams were prophetic in some way. After all, Othala had confirmed Torfar was indeed still alive.

She felt Romarin's gaze and turned to face him. He looked concerned. "What's wrong?" she asked.

"You have a very serious expression," Romarin said. "Do you wish to share?"

Kalena shrugged. "Last night, I saw Cahal again. He said I could see him because I was so close to death."

Romarin nodded. "Sometimes that happens, but more often to first-bloods than any other, or so I've been told."

"But I'm not a first-blood," Kalena said. "Nor was Cahal. And yet, he told me about Torfar. Don't you find that odd?"

Romarin shook his head. "Not really."

"Why not? I have no connection to the Wyrd."

"Ah, but that is where you are wrong," Romarin said. "Everything is connected to the Wyrd. It is the past, the present and the future. Nothing can exist without the Wyrd – and you are most certainly as tied to it as I am."

"But I'm Wyrd-blind. I have no magic and certainly not the Sight."

Romarin shrugged. "Cahal wasn't first-blood, and yet, he could use mindspeak just like a first-blood. Whatever strengths we have we must build on them, Kally. Your strength is being the warrior you are."

Kalena shrugged. She drank the tea and stared at the spitted meat

hanging over the fire. She wasn't hungry any longer, but she was feeling stiff and sore. She stood up and stretched slowly. "I could use some
practice before my fingers get numb again," she said.

Romarin raised an eyebrow. "You feel up to it?"

"I feel fine," Kalena said. She stepped away and drew her sword,
swinging it slowly. After all the fights with the fireworms, the riding on
Othala and the mind-numbing cold, Kalena's muscles felt stiff and rigid
– she wouldn't have the reflexes she needed if another fireworm attacked.
As she swung the sword, she felt her cramped muscles loosen and began
one of the sword katas Cahal had taught her many years before.

The kata was simple. It was a stylistic set of movements intended
to teach the student the correct moves while fighting. There were other
katas in sword, staff and empty-hand, but the one she chose was inter-
mediate. Enough to work her out easily, but not enough to overstrain
herself. There were usually two players in this kata: a master and pupil.
Since she had no master, she took the role, herself, and practiced against
an unseen opponent.

She used the kata to focus on her breathing and to relax her muscles
between movements. As she did, she felt her muscles warm and loosen.
When she finished, she bowed to the imaginary opponent in respect and
as she raised her head, she saw Romarin bowing to her.

"Again?" he asked.

"Do you know this kata?"

Romarin grinned. "It's been some years. Please, take the master's role."

Kalena hesitated. She had not expected to train with the king, but did
not object. She bowed once and began the kata.

The kata was simple enough, starting with the eager pupil who
attacked, while the master parried and watched. Eventually, the master
took advantage of the enthusiasm and slowly forced the pupil to learn
from it. Romarin started with the few simple cuts; Kalena parried them
with ease. She responded with the prescribed attack, only to have Romarin
step aside from the attack and try to cut her hand underneath.

Kalena responded with a quick parry and raised and eyebrow. *Didn't
he remember the kata?* she wondered. Something in his eyes told her he did
and that now, he simply wanted swordplay. She tested her theory and
started with several quick thrusts to the head and arms. Romarin parried
and she swung the sword low to cut at his legs. Romarin backed off and
began to circle.

A smile formed on Kalena's lips, despite herself. Romarin's style spoke of Cahal's influences and she recognized the attacks as they came towards her. She grinned, parrying them easily and offered counterattacks. Romarin recognized those and parried as well.

The last time she had fought against Romarin, it had been very close to a real combat situation. While it had been until first blood, the reality was that drawing blood without seriously injuring took more finesse than simple practice sparring or actual combat. In the heady rush of the trials, she had been only looking to find an opening to make that score. Like battle, it wasn't intended to continue for long.

But practice sparring was much different. Unlike actual combat, it had a rhythm to it. Cut, parry, thrust. Slice, block, counter. Each set of movements was strong and deliberate. Cahal trained the basics by rote. Constant training became instinctive and when faced with a particular attack, one's body would be ready with the counter. Cahal taught that way because in the heat of battle, fear could take over and numb the intellect, but the body, trained to recognize so many attacks, could defend itself and launch a counterattack automatically.

Romarin attacked in a series of thrusts Kalena knew well. But this time, she stepped aside and launched into another attack, instead of defending herself. Romarin's blade almost hit her shoulder, but she twisted and clipped his left elbow with the flat of her blade. Romarin yelped, more in surprise than pain and reached out, lightning-fast with his gauntleted hand. Kalena was ready for it and snicked the blade upward, slapping his triceps.

Romarin looked shocked at first and then began to laugh. "I suppose I deserved that," he said, sheathing his sword and rubbing his sore arm.

"You did deserve it," Kalena agreed. "Don't try the same trick twice on the same opponents. They always learn from their first mistake, if they live." She grinned. "I learned my lesson well from the trials."

Romarin chuckled. "I suppose you're..." He halted and never finished the sentence. Instead, he looked upward towards the cliffs.

"What is it?" Kalena asked.

An all too familiar scream echoed in the valley.

Chapter Thirty-Nine

It was late afternoon and the sun had crested the hills, but Kalena recognized the dark shape of a fireworm flying towards them. Even if the fireworm didn't know they were there, it would smell the cooking meat and see the wisps of smoke rise from the valley floor.

Kalena turned and ran to the fire, kicking dirt and snow into the embers.

"Don't bother with that!" Romarin ordered. "Get your bow."

Kalena doubted that she would have another lucky shot, but grasped her bow and strung it after sheathing her sword. She nocked an arrow, but saw that Romarin was shouldering the packs and what food and blankets he could gather. "We're not fighting?"

"Not unless we have to – come on!" Romarin led the way deeper into the forest. Kalena followed, trying to keep her gaze on the treetops and on the path at the same time. The pace that Romarin set made it impossible and she found she couldn't hear much above the pounding of her own heart as she ran after him. Her legs and lungs burned as she pushed herself harder still. She noted they were heading up towards the knife-edge where Othala had told them to go but beyond that, she didn't know how Romarin knew the way.

Twice she thought she heard the fireworm screams over her hammering heart. She slipped and scrambled on the steep slopes. Romarin quickened his pace each time. The snow grew deeper too under the shelter of the dark pines. What had been ankle deep snow quickly became knee deep. The forest's canopy grew thicker until they were thrown into near twilight and Kalena couldn't see the sky.

It was here, Romarin halted. He stuck his sword into the snow point first and leaned against a tree, panting. Kalena too, was gasping for breath, but she dared not collapse, despite her aching legs. Running through the deep snow had exhausted them both and Kalena's lungs burned with each breath she took.

"We're safe," Romarin said, between gasps of air. Kalena looked at his face – it was beet red from exertion. She suspected her own face was that color as well. How far had they run? Kalena looked down the hill. She guessed the camp was three miles or more away. How they had managed to run with packs and armor, uphill in the rarified air made her pause.

"How do we know it won't follow us?" Kalena asked; her voice unsteady between each raspy breath.

Romarin shook his head. "I don't hear it anymore. I think it went away."

"Didn't it smell our fire?"

"I don't know."

Kalena looked at Romarin in puzzlement, but there was no jest in either his face or voice. Just exhaustion. For the first time in quite a while, he looked vulnerable to her. Perhaps it was something as simple as his admission that he didn't know if the fireworm had been after them, or whether it was seeing him panting and as worn out as she was, she realized just how much he relied on her as she was relying on him. He had saved her life, yes, but she had taken down worms alongside him. Cahal had told her many times Romarin needed a guide. Cahal had thought her that guide.

The thought was sobering. She was just a *Chi'lan*, and yet, was Rhyn'athel calling her to do greater things? Her conversation with the god had faded from her memory, and yet, somehow it seemed right.

She ruminated on that for a while until her breath slowed enough for her not to sound so winded. Although she couldn't see the sky, the deepening shadows suggested the sun had already passed the hills and was setting. "We have to go," she said. "We're not safe here."

Romarin looked at her and nodded. "Where do you think we can find shelter?" His voice too was stronger and his complexion was less ruddy.

Kalena looked around. The narrow valleys would provide the most chance for finding natural shelter that were uninhabited by fireworms, but their path lay upward towards the danger. "I don't know," she said. "There may be some caves once we get above tree line."

"That would leave us exposed," Romarin said.

"I know. I just don't want to go back down to the valley. We must be close to the knife-edge by now."

Romarin made no reply. Kalena started walking slowly uphill in an effort to see the knife-edge. To her surprise, Romarin followed. She crested the ridge and found an opening that enabled her to see the knife-edge. With that, her hopes sank.

She was looking at was the front side of the knife-edge. A thousand feet beyond where they stood, the mountain turned into a sheer face, where there was no way to climb it.

"How could we get up there?" Kalena asked, looking at the rock. She was dubious they could scale the cliffs without ropes or climbing equipment.

Romarin's steady gaze met hers. "What would you suggest?"

Kalena surveyed the cliff. "Maybe there's an easier way around this rock – a path or maybe something that wouldn't require equipment."

Romarin shook his head. "Regardless, it's too late to start. Let's find some shelter – or build it."

Kalena frowned. From what she could see, there was little natural shelter in the form of caves and the ground along the ridge was snowy and wet. Still, she nodded. "Let's follow the ridgeline a bit. If we don't find anything that'll make decent shelter, we'll have to make another lean-to."

Romarin nodded in assent and let her lead the way. Kalena trudged through the calf-high drifts, her leather boots becoming soaked, despite the wax and oil coatings, and her feet growing wet. She wanted a hot fire and hot soup, or maybe even methglyn, but she knew she wouldn't get either.

Walking uphill through the snow was tiring, too. She found herself taking several steps and then stopping to catch her breath. Looking at Romarin, she could see that even with his first-blood constitution, the altitude and the work affected him, too.

After a half hour, the ridge leveled out and the walk became easier, but no less cold. The snow was less deep, but the wind had picked up. Despite the padded gambeson and cloak, the wind seemed to cut into her skin. Her face felt raw. Kalena looked to Romarin in askance, but he seemed lost in thought. Kalena stopped.

"What's wrong?" Romarin asked.

"This is it," she said. "We're not going any farther tonight."

Romarin frowned and Kalena could see the doubt on his face. "The wind is bad here," he said.

"It won't be any better the higher up we go," she argued. "And if we get to a lee, we're going to find snow drifts." She fell silent, watching the king. She thought for a moment Romarin would argue, but instead, he smiled slightly and unshouldered the packs.

"Fine, let's stay here then."

It took them almost an hour to cut enough branches and enough boughs to make a suitable lean-to. The ground was very hard and cold here and Kalena had no desire to have the warmth sapped from her body, so she worked at cutting boughs with her dagger. The wind was persistent, blowing across her face and through her short hair. With each new gust, Kalena cursed the wind gods for their torment.

Romarin busied himself with finding downed logs for the lean-to's frame. They had no rope to tie the logs together so Romarin had to hack notches into the wood with his dagger so that it would fit together. Kalena frowned as she watched him. Both their daggers were getting dull from the work. As the shadows deepened, Kalena had laid the boughs on the ground and covered them with the blanket. Romarin had finished the lean-to and Kalena added extra boughs for wind protection.

After finishing the lean-to, she was surprised to see Romarin arranging a pile of wood, twigs and pine needles for a fire. "Won't we summon the fireworms?" she asked as he struck the flint against his dagger.

Romarin shrugged. "If we don't have a fire, we'll be dead by morning on this hill anyway. It's too cold here without one."

As night fell, the wind stopped. Despite her reservations, the fire proved to be a morale booster for her. As Romarin warmed some water in a cup, she speared what was left of the elk meat and reheated it. Kalena smiled as he handed her the cup to drink, after taking a long drink, himself.

"What I wouldn't give for hot mead," Kalena said.

"Mead," Romarin repeated with a snort. "I'd settle for a warm bed."

Kalena chuckled and then looked into the sky. She could see patches of it beyond the canopy. "I wonder how the others are faring in Citadel Heights."

Romarin closed his eyes. "I don't know. I may not have a kingdom to go back to."

Kalena looked away. "Do you like being king?" she wondered aloud. As soon as she said it, she gasped at her boldness.

To her surprise, Romarin chuckled. "It's all right, Kally."

"You're not angry?"

"Kally, you saved my life several times already. Do you really think I would be angry at that question?"

Kalena gave a noncommittal shrug.

"I became king because there was no one else," he said. "Because I was expected to be king."

"But you had a challenger."

"Yes, I did," Romarin took the cup from her and put more snow in it to melt on the fire. "But, I am the son of Rhyn'athel. I was raised to be Nevfaras' heir, even though I was not his son. Being a son of a god has expectations thrust on you."

"I'd imagine so," Kalena said. She meant it, even though her words came out quickly. "I mean, that's a lot to bear." She paused. "Krysa could've saved you a lot of anguish by keeping your birthright a secret."

Romarin chuckled.

"What?"

"You've seen Rhyn'athel, do you think my father's identity would remain secret for long?"

Kalena was about to reply when she caught movement in the corner of her eye. She turned her head and stared into the forest. Two blue, glowing eyes gazed back at her.

Chapter Forty

Kalena stood up, drawing her blade, but no sooner had she moved, than the glowing eyes disappeared. She stared into the dark forest, scanning for anything present, but there was nothing. The wind had picked up again, causing the boughs to sway in an odd dance.

Romarin scrambled to his feet. He stood a few paces behind her. His left hand gripped the hilt of his own sword as he waited for her to move.

:*What did you see?* he asked in mindspeak.

:*I thought I saw eyes – just for a moment*, Kalena replied. She shivered involuntarily despite herself.

If Romarin didn't believe her, he said nothing. Instead, they stood for a long time looking around. When it was obvious that the creature was nowhere in sight, Kalena sighed and lowered her weapon. "I saw something."

Romarin patted her shoulder. "You might have seen a deer or even one of those snow leopards."

Kalena frowned. "I don't like the idea of having a predator so close."

"Nor do I," Romarin said. "We can take turns at the watch, if you'd like."

Kalena nodded. "I'll take the first watch."

They ate the elk meat in silence, scanning the forest for any signs of movement. But neither of them saw anything and Romarin paused at the entrance to the lean-to. "I can take the first watch," he offered.

Kalena shook her head. "I can't sleep right now," she said. "We're so close to the knife-edge."

"Wake me in three hours. Be sure that you keep the fire going; if that was a snow leopard, it's unlikely to attack us while there's a fire." With that, he crawled under the blankets in the lean-to.

Kalena took a stick and poked the fire with it to stir the embers. The flames danced, sending a small shower of sparks into the air. Kalena frowned, chagrinned. The fire would keep away the ground predators, but might attract the fireworms. She now wished she was anywhere but here. She wondered what Cahal would think of her cowardice.

In her mind's eye, she could see the old *Chi'lan* laughing at her. She missed him terribly. She wished he were there to offer advice or at least support. Even so, she wondered if he had truly appeared in her dreams to tell her of Torfar.

Torfar. Her mind settled on the name. What kind of man turned from his *Chi'lan* vow to betray his king? The *Chi'lan* warriors were not perfect and there had been traitors throughout history, for mortals were still lured by greed and ambition. Kalena tried to understand Torfar's reasons behind betraying the *Chi'lan* and their new king. Torfar was a first-blood, like Romarin. Torfar, of all *Lochvaur*, would know what it meant to be *Chi'lan*.

Kalena shook her head. She didn't understand why and couldn't understand why Allarun would've let Torfar live. Nothing made sense to her.

She continued to add wood to the fire and spent her watch listening to the wind and creaking of trees. Occasionally, she'd hear Romarin's breathing or shifting in the lean-to, but heard and saw nothing else. She watched the sky as the first moon appeared overhead. She stood up and stretched and gently woke Romarin for the watch. She then settled into the blankets, already warmed by Romarin's body heat and fell fast asleep.

It wasn't long before Kalena awoke to Romarin shaking her. It was still dark in the lean-to and the first moon, Tomah, was still overhead. She gasped but saw Romarin put his finger to his lips. :*Something is out there*, he said in mindspeak. :*Get your bow.*

Romarin pulled away, but Kalena could see he had his sword in hand. She scrambled out of the warm lean-to and strung the bow, nocking it with an arrow. As she did, she caught a glimpse of blue eyes glint just outside the firelight. She thought she heard a growl like a low rumble emanate from the creature.

Kalena needed no encouragement. Despite her cold hands, she drew back the arrow and let it loose. The arrow sped towards the eyes, but at the last moment, the eyes disappeared. She heard the arrow bury into the snow. She looked at Romarin in askance, but the king was silent, scanning the area for anything.

"What was it?" she whispered.

Romarin shook his head. :*I don't know — I can't sense it with the Sight.*

Kalena frowned. She wasn't prepared for that answer. She continued to scan the area, but saw nothing. As she began to grow tired, she felt Romarin's hand on her arm.

"Go to bed," he said softly. "Leave the bow with me."

Kalena nodded, her mind dulled with exhaustion. She crawled back inside the lean-to and fell into an uneasy sleep.

Chapter Forty-One

Lachlan drew Uruz, letting the power of the Sword of Destiny flow through him. He knew without looking that Elsonre had drawn Eihwaz and Allarun had drawn Hagalaz. He waited for Silvain to approach before brandishing Uruz. The Sword of Destiny glowed with power.

Silvain blanched at the Sword and met Lachlan's gaze. "This is not how I would come to you," he said gruffly.

Lachlan smiled. "I imagine not."

"I do so only on the urging of my nobles," he said. "We would've fought you to the very end, but my counsel thinks it is better to make peace or lose what is left of my people."

"We have been at war much too long," Lachlan said. "It is time for peace. Give me your sword."

"Return my daughter."

Lachlan glanced at Cara and smiled grimly. "That, I cannot do."

"Then, there will be no peace." Silvain spat on the ground at Lachlan's feet.

Lachlan smiled slightly. "It is her choice, Silvain, but I think she has already made it. Cara?"

Kalena stepped forward. "I am a Chi'lan, father. I have always been; you know this. My heart is with Lachlan and I would marry no other. I am sorry I have put you through such anguish."

The pain in Silvain's eyes was intense. He closed them. "I have no child and no heir."

The morning sun shone bright on her face as Kalena awoke. Despite the lean-to and the boughs covering it, a small shaft of sunlight played upon her face. The cold air and the smell of the fire crackling nearby surprised her. She had overslept. Romarin had either not awakened her or something had happened during the night. A cold stab of panic ran through her as she remembered the glowing eyes, and she scrambled out of the lean-to.

"Romarin?" She looked around. The sun was bright against her face and for the first time, she got a good look at her surroundings. The place they chose for the lean-to wasn't nearly as covered as she thought in the twilight. Through the thin canopy overhead, the sky was a beautiful sapphire blue. "Romarin?" Her words caught in her throat as she wheeled around and, to her surprise, collided into him as he came behind her. She bounced off his chest with a whuff noise and nearly fell, but he caught her and held her.

"Kalena? Are you all right?" Romarin's eyes were concerned, but something else glittered in them. Amusement? Kalena realized how close she was to him and tried backing up, only he was holding her firmly.

"I'm fine," she said, irritation creeping into her voice. "Where were you?"

Romarin laughed. "I thought I'd relieve myself."

Kalena flushed, much to her surprise. But her embarrassment quickly turned to ire. "Why didn't you wake me up for the next watch?"

"I couldn't sleep," Romarin said. "You were sleeping so peacefully, I thought I'd let you get some rest." He looked at her in puzzlement. "Are you angry?" He released her.

"Yes, I was worried about you when I didn't see you. The creature last night..."

"Ah." He shook his head. "The animal, whatever it was, didn't come back."

Kalena's eyes narrowed. She felt angry, but didn't really know why. Romarin was safe and that's what she was worried about, wasn't she? Then, why was she angry? She didn't have an answer. She clenched her fists and then turned to the fire, deciding to kneel down and rub her cold hands before it. Her emotions were all roiled up inside her and she felt confused. What was she feeling towards Romarin? She didn't really know.

Romarin knelt down beside her. "Kally..."

"Don't call me that."

Kalena glared at the flames. She had never been so worried over anyone before. Even Cahal and Lochalan, the two men who were her family, had never evoked this response from her. She could feel Romarin's gaze on her and she knew he was sorely tempted to try to read her mind, but dared not, lest she sense him.

Go on, she goaded him. *Just try.* She fixed her gaze and her thoughts on the fire.

"Kalena," Romarin's voice was barely a whisper. "What's wrong?"

Kalena took a slow, steady breath. *What was wrong with her? Why was she so confused?*

It was the dream.

With sudden clarity, Kalena looked at Romarin. Lachlan's visage was still strong in her mind and she looked at the king with a critical eye. She shook her head and smiled ruefully. "Nothing, Romarin."

Romarin cocked his head, obviously not seeing what she had. "Are you sure?"

"As certain as I can be," she said. She smiled sadly. "Let's find the knife-edge." With that, she stood and brushed herself off, leaving Romarin more perplexed.

Chapter Forty-Two

They had broken camp and began walking westward along the cliffs. The rock was less jagged here and the slope less severe. The trees fell away from the rough, gravel slopes and Kalena felt exposed and small against the massive snowfields and barren rocks. But there was nowhere else to go.

Othala had steered them true when she said they'd be safer along this route. The fireworm caves were east of where they stood and Kalena couldn't see them from here. Even so, she could hear the screams and clacks coming from the caves and occasionally see a black shape flit from the other side. Each time she saw the creatures, she held her breath, hoping that they didn't see them.

Romarin's face was grim when he saw the fireworms. :*I hope they can't see us this far.*

Kalena mentally agreed, but wondered what the fireworms' eyesight was like. She knew the big hawks and eagles could see several miles. She suspected the fireworms and dragons had a similar type of vision.

Kalena hoped there would be a way to the top of the knife-edge. They walked cautiously, keeping their eyes on the fireworms' lairs and on the skies. Kalena occasionally glanced around, feeling as though something else was watching them. Her mind went back to Othala's warning over the snow leopards. She wondered if what she saw was indeed one of those wild cats.

There was no cover here, nor were there any way for them to seek cover if the fireworms saw them. Their cloaks stood out bright red against the snow and dark rocks. Kalena grimaced as she looked at Romarin and then down at herself. Her surcoat, while tattered and stained dark with blood from the battles, still stood out in this desolate place.

She turned to Romarin. "Your cloak and surcoat," she said. "Take them off."

Romarin paused. "Why?"

"The red makes us a target," she said. "The fireworms will see us even from this distance."

Romarin chuckled as he pulled the surcoat and cloak off. "Good thinking. Perhaps we should consider uniforms that will camouflage us in the future."

As Kalena pulled her cloak off, she felt the cold seep into her through the gambeson. She carefully folded it and the surcoat up and stowed it in her pack. "I wish we had darker cloaks."

"If we get cold, we might use the blankets," Romarin said. He glanced at her. "But I wonder if the adamantine might attract the worms as well."

"We're both pretty dirty and our mail is tarnished, so I think we'll be safe enough."

Kalena led the way. She searched for a path along the rocks and boulder fields, hoping to find a trail or at least a way through towards the cliff heights. She had expected Romarin to lead, but instead, he deferred to her skill and followed. The ground became steeper and snow-covered as they continued their ascent. The sun slowly rose in the eastern sky on the two climbers. There was no sign of fireworms on this side of the mountain – possibly because the creatures didn't expect anyone to try to scale their lairs.

Morning became noon and still Kalena and Romarin climbed. Kalena found herself gasping in the rarified air, exhausted from the exertion, lack of food, and dehydration. She motioned for Romarin to stop as she sat down beside a glacier and scooped up a handful of clean snow. She had emptied her canteen an hour before.

The snow provided little water to her parched throat, but anything was better than nothing, Kalena decided. The cold wind that had provided some relief in their exertion now cut through them. While the padded arming shirt and leggings offered some insulation, they were soaked with sweat and caused her to shiver involuntarily. Romarin sat beside her as she scanned the cliffs. The knife-edge ridge connected the mountain they were on to the high bluffs. Traversable, she thought, but with the afternoon coming on, Kalena didn't like being so exposed. A glint from their mail, as dirty as it might be, might still attract the fire-worms. Still, she didn't see any other way.

Kalena turned and noticed that Romarin was studying her. "I think we should go along the knife-edge," she said. "It's the only way unless you see an alternative I haven't."

Romarin's steel eyes considered the knife-edge. "Dangerous," he stated. "We'll have to wait until dark."

"Night – on the knife-edge?" Kalena said. "I can see well in the dark, but all it takes is one slip. And we can't stay here in the wind – we'll freeze."

"What would you suggest, *Chi'lan?*" Romarin asked steadily.

Kalena hesitated, her silver eyes darted to the knife-edge. *Was there another way? Did Romarin know something she did not? Was this a test?* For a moment, the questions and uncertainty flooded her mind. She scanned the land again, looking for a hidden pass. But there was none.

"The knife-edge," she said, holding his gaze with her own; her voice steady. "We have to cross now – we can't risk a night crossing. Tomah and Iamar will rise tonight – the moons will give enough light for the fireworms to see us, negating any possible concealment." She paused. "Either that or we climb down now and find an alternate route."

Romarin nodded. "The shadows will be lengthening within the hour. We may be able to avoid detection if the other mountains throw us into shadow."

"Maybe," Kalena said. She rose, despite the strong wind. "We've got to keep moving if we don't want to freeze up here."

It took them nearly an hour to make their way to the jagged ridge. When Kalena got there, she stopped and stared. It was not a true knife-edge, having about a half foot to a foot of traversable ground before the cliff fell away precipitously on either side. The wind had scoured the edge of any snow, but Kalena noted that a slight film of ice had formed. "Gods," she muttered as she put one foot on the icy path. One bad step would end their lives.

"Wait," said Romarin. "Do you still have your dagger?"

Kalena halted but did not turn around for fear she might slip. "Yes."

"Take it out," he said, "and hold it in your right hand. If you slip, you may be able to use it to arrest your fall."

"Good thinking," said Kalena, pulling the dagger from her belt. She walked forward carefully, listening for Romarin as he walked slowly behind her. The knife-edge was slow going, but Kalena continued to walk forward. Her confidence increased with each step.

A scream echoed across the mountain faces. Kalena froze, not daring to glance behind. The scream was mammalian, not reptilian.

:*Snow leopard*, spoke Romarin's voice in her mind. :*Keep moving.*

Kalena glanced behind. Romarin was about 15 feet behind her. :*Where is it?*

:*I don't know—keep moving.*

Kalena took a few more steps and the scream resounded over the cliffs. :*By Rhyn'athel's sword, if that creature continues screaming, it's likely to call a fireworm.*

Another scream. Closer yet.

:*Run!* Romarin's voice exploded in her head.

Kalena gasped and leapt forward, nearly slipping on the ice. She crossed the last twenty feet and halted as she heard a violent scream. She turned to see Romarin struggling against a white snow leopard with saber fangs. Somehow, the king had managed to stay on the knife-edge – Kalena realized he must have seen the cat and braced for the impact. The cat was about the size of a puma, but it had thick white fur and a strange mottling that gave it camouflage against the snow and rock. Its claws buried into Romarin's back. Romarin held the cat by the throat with his silver gauntleted hand and held the dagger in the other. He plunged the knife into the cat, only to be thrown off balance and began sliding off the knife-edge.

Chapter Forty-Three

"Romarin!" Kalena shouted. The cat toppled off and tumbled down the knife-edge with a loud screech. Romarin skittered on the ice and fell, barely catching himself with a gauntleted hand. Without thinking, Kalena charged across the knife-edge and knelt down on the thin lip of rock. She grasped Romarin by his left wrist and slowly pulled him up.

A fireworm screamed overhead. Kalena swore and turned in time to see the creature racing towards them. She slashed at the worm with her dagger as it made a pass at them with outstretched talons. Kalena nearly lost her balance, but Romarin caught her.

:*Come on*, Romarin tugged at her.

They both ran to the opposite side and stepped onto a wide ledge. The fireworm circled, this time breathing fire at them. Kalena winced, but Romarin had already anticipated the creature's move and a bright blue wall of energy deflected the fire. The fireworm screeched and Kalena drew her sword, ready for battle.

:*No*, said Romarin. :*This way*.

Romarin led Kalena across the ledge. To her surprise, there was a door hewn in the rock. They both ran inside and halted.

Kalena stared in wonder. They stood within a vast cavern filled with gold, adamantine, and gems, each piled in mounds, just as she remembered from her dream. Armor, swords, and other weapons lay strewn across the hoard and glittered in the dim light. For there was light -- the walls glowed from some luminescent source that Kalena could not discern. Kalena turned to Romarin in wonder.

"I thought dragons hoarded gold," she said.

Romarin shook his head. "Dragons care little for these trinkets," he replied. "Fireworms are the hoarders. Because fireworms are cousins to dragons, it's little wonder there's some confusion, but you'll insult Othala if you ever made that mistake to her face."

"I'll keep that in mind," Kalena remarked. She walked forward gazing at the treasure in wonder. "There must be tons of treasure here."

"Indeed."

Kalena turned. "Where do you think Cahal is?"

Romarin didn't answer, his silver eyes fixed on something lying on one of the mounds. He strode to the mound and picked it up. It was a long sword. His face was grim. "*Fyren.*"

Kalena stood beside him, tears filling her eyes as he handed the blade to her. *Fyren* was a magnificent blade: glowing silver adamantine and adorned with runes. She lowered her head and began to weep silently. She couldn't help herself, now that she knew for certain that Cahal was really dead. Cahal would not part with that blade, except in death.

:Don't cry, Kally, a voice echoed in her mind. Kalena looked up and for a brief instant, saw Cahal standing beside her. His ghostly hand rested on her shoulder. *:I am in the Hall of the Gods, where I should've been a long time before.*

"Then, why can I see you?" she asked as she rubbed her eyes.

Romarin looked nonplused. "What?" He turned around to look at her. "Of course you can see me." He laid *Fyren* at his feet.

Kalena looked at Cahal in askance. Her old mentor shook his head. *:He can't see me, Kally, only you can.*

"Why?"

:Because that is how the magic is.

"What's going on?" Romarin asked. "Who are you talking to?"

Kalena felt Romarin's mental nudge and pushed back. "It's Cahal, he's here."

Concerned flashed in Romarin's eyes as he scanned the cavern and then back to Kalena. "I don't see him."

"He says you can't – that's how the magic works." She shrugged. She turned to Cahal. "What now?"

:You don't have much time – Torfar will be here soon. Take up Fyren and both you and Romarin may be able to kill him. Kill Torfar and the fireworm attacks will end.

Kalena knelt down and picked up the adamantine blade that Cahal once carried. "Can *Fyren* kill Torfar?" She cradled the sword in her hands, noting the dark stain along the blood groove.

:This is the sword that wounded the death god, himself, Cahal replied. *:It is more powerful than Torfar. Only Torfar had me at a disadvantage when he killed me.*

Romarin looked from Kalena to where Cahal stood. Kalena knew he couldn't quite see Cahal, but she suspected that with his first-blood powers, he sensed Cahal's presence. "Cahal," Romarin said softly. "I can barely sense you – why?"

:*Tell Romarin that of all the warriors, you, Kally can defeat Torfar.*

"That makes no sense," Kalena murmured. She turned to Romarin. "He says that only I can defeat Torfar."

:*That, I would like to see.*

Both turned to see the ugliest fireworm Kalena had ever seen.

Chapter Forty-Four

What Kalena and Romarin saw was a fireworm entering the cavern from the other side. It was a large creature, nearly seventy feet long with pale, translucent skin and red eyes. Kalena stared. This monster was unlike any fireworm she had ever seen. As fierce and ugly as it was, its eyes held a cunning she had never seen in other worms. *Sentient intelligence*, she thought.

She looked to Cahal whose face was a mask of anger. :*Torfar.*

"Torfar?" she repeated. "How could this be? This is a fireworm, not a wizard."

"Torfar," Romarin said, his eyes steeling at the fireworm's appearance. He drew his sword. "What happened to Cahal?"

:*I dispatched Cahal easily enough after he slew my second-in-command*, the worm replied. :*Pity that Cahal killed that worm – he was one of the larger ones in these lairs.*

"You were a *Chi'lan* warrior like us. What happened?" Kalena asked.

:*Why don't you ask Romarin what his stepfather, Nevfaras, did to me all those many years ago?*

Romarin stared at Torfar in bewilderment and shook his head. "You betrayed my foster-father and turned him over to Allarun. You sold Nevfaras to Allarun for gold."

:*Nevfaras was a fool*, the worm hissed. :*He would've died by Allarun's hand eventually...*

"You betrayed a *Chi'lan* and your king," Romarin said. "You broke your oath to Rhyn'athel."

:*But Nevfaras did exact vengeance*, Cahal said to Kalena. :*Though not gifted with the first-blood powers, he was a powerful Chi'lan and beloved of Rhyn'athel. His death curse made Torfar into what you see now.*

Kalena gazed at Torfar. "Nevfaras cursed you, didn't he?" she said, raising *Fyren*. "And you became that which your heart already was – a worm."

"A death curse, of course," Romarin said. "Nevfaras cursed you for your betrayal. Spoken by the one man who would've readily given his life for your pitiful existence."

"You've been sending the fireworms after us, haven't you?" Kalena demanded, raising *Fyren* in a defensive position. "As our punishment for Nevfaras' curse – a curse that you brought upon yourself!"

:*What is this, Romarin? Your hussy?* the fireworm said scornfully.

Romarin smiled grimly. "A *Chi'lan* warrior."

The fireworm laughed – a harsh grating sound that caused Kalena to suppress a shudder. :*What? This girl? You've gotten desperate, Romarin, if you're relying on girls to fight for you.*

With a yell, Kalena charged forward, swinging *Fyren*.

"Kalena! No! I can't protect you!" Romarin shouted, but Kalena was already running towards the worm.

For Lochalan. For her parents. For Cahal. For Nevfaras. For everyone this evil creature had destroyed.

Torfar reared and opened his maw. Flames shot towards her before Kalena realized what was happening. But before they hit her, something passed between her and Torfar. Cahal had stepped between them and raised his hands as though to ward off the fireworm's breath. A blue light encircled Kalena, protecting her.

She saw her teacher grin, and she almost laughed in incredulity. "I thought you had no magic."

:*That has changed since I entered the Hall of the Gods*, Cahal said. :*Get him, Kally. Show the traitor how a real Chi'lan fights.*

Torfar leapt at her, his massive jaws snapping. Kalena barely had time to react as the great beast came at her. She leapt aside and swung *Fyren* down onto the worm's scaly flesh. Torfar shrieked as the battle blade bit through scales and into muscle and sinew. Black blood poured from the wound and he shook his head violently, wrenching the sword from Kalena's grasp.

But Romarin was right beside her and plunged his own blade into the fireworm. It shot flames at Romarin, but he deflected them with his own magic. Torfar shook *Fyren* loose and it clattered to the ground. Kalena drew her own sword now and ran under Torfar's belly as he turned to attack Romarin. As she bent down, the fireworm's tail came around and knocked her to the ground. But she now had *Fyren*.

The familiar coppery taste of blood filled Kalena's mouth as she sat up, gripping the blade in both hands. Kalena felt dizzy, and as she stood up, felt like retching, but she forced herself to focus on the battle between Romarin and Torfar.

Torfar had wrapped part of his coils around the king. Romarin held the fireworm's head back, gripping the creature's throat with his silver gauntleted hand. Claws raked down Romarin's body and still, he held on, his gauntlet closing on the fireworm's throat. The creature thrashed, rolling and throwing Romarin off his feet, threatening to crush him.

"Romarin!" Kalena yelled and leapt into the fray. She took the sword and slammed it point down through the coils and into the solid stone. Flames shot from the sword and ran through the length of the worm. Romarin struggled and pulled himself from the coils. With a last effort, Kalena swung *Fyren* and it bit through spine, snapping Torfar's neck. For a moment, Kalena thought she saw Cahal beside her, wielding a ghostly version of *Fyren*. But, when she turned her head, he was gone.

Torfar collapsed. Romarin released his sword as it clattered to the ground. He then dropped to his knees. Kalena ran to his side. "Romarin!" she said and halted in dismay.

The damage was overwhelming. The worm's talons had raked across his back, tearing the armor like paper. Long gashes ran down his arms and legs and she could see one large wound in his chest. Romarin was coughing blood and his face was ashen. "Kalena," he whispered. "*Fyren…*"

"I have it."

"Bring it here," he whispered. "I may be able to use it, but I need your strength."

Kalena knelt beside him. "What do I do?"

"I don't have enough strength to heal myself," he said. "But you do."

"How – I have no magic."

"Hold *Fyren* between us. I can use the sword's power as a conduit and use your strength to heal me."

Kalena nodded. She held the sword out. Romarin placed his hands on the blade. *Fyren* began to glow. Slowly, she could feel her strength flow from herself to Romarin. Wounds closed. Blood stopped flowing. Kalena felt dizzy, but still gripped the sword. A wave of nausea filled her. For a moment, she gazed into Romarin's silver eyes and saw that his face was returning to its normal color. Then, she blacked out.

Chapter Forty-Five

The darkness was overwhelming. Kalena could see nothing and yet, she was conscious of someone standing beside her.

"Romarin?"

"No," came Cahal's voice.

Kalena blinked and suddenly she was standing on the parapet of a great castle, overlooking impossibly green fields and into a sapphire-blue sky. The light from the twin suns nearly blinded her as she leaned against the merlon and looked into her old mentor's face. They were both dressed in clean clothes, bearing the mark of Rhyn'athel, the warrior god. Cahal was grinning at her, and to her surprise, she was grinning right back.

"It's beautiful, isn't it?" Cahal said. "Rhyn told me about Athelren years ago, but his description doesn't even do it justice."

"We're in Athelren?" she gasped. "I'm dead?"

"No, you're not." Cahal began chuckling. "You're unconscious, and Rhyn let me see my favorite pupil one last time to say goodbye."

"Goodbye?" she whispered. "I'll never see you again?"

"Not until you finally return to Athelren," he said, "but you have a long life ahead of you before you do."

"I've missed you," she said.

"I know," he said. "And I have missed you. So has Lochalan."

"Is he here?" she asked suddenly.

"Yes, but Rhyn'athel has limited your contact to just me," Cahal said. "Lochalan is fine and he's proud of you."

To her surprise, she felt tears roll down her face. "Sorry."

"Kally," Cahal said and tipped her chin upward. "Don't cry. You and Romarin have destroyed a great evil. Your people are now free of the fireworm scourge."

"Romarin, is he all right?"

"He's fine. Right now, he's caring for you. He loves you very much."

Kalena closed her eyes and turned away, a knot growing in her stomach. "Is he Lachlan's incarnation?"

"What do you think?"

Kalena turned back around and cocked her head slightly. "You can't tell me, can you?"

"No, but honestly, Kally, I don't know the entire future, nor how it will play out."

"Can you tell me if he's the one?" she asked. "He loves me, I know, and yet..."

"And yet there's a hesitancy," Cahal finished. He sighed and the grin returned. "I think I can at least tell you that. Is he to be your love? No."

Kalena sighed. Hearing Cahal's words made her feel as though a great burden had been lifted from her. "Then, there will be another."

"Yes, and who knows? He may even be a half-blood mercenary."

She laughed and then grew serious. "I'm not going to remember this, am I?"

Cahal nodded. "You'll remember we talked and said farewell. You may have a feeling from time to time that something I've said seems familiar. But not much more than that." He paused. "Take care of Fyren. It was Lochvaur's blade which was passed to great warriors such as Lachlei, Lachlan and, yes, myself. It has no magic, save it was forged from adamantine from this world." He hugged her. "Make me proud, my foster-daughter."

Kalena kissed Cahal on the cheek, and then her world spun into darkness.

"Kalena."

Kalena awoke to Romarin's voice and found herself lying beside a small fire in a forest. She was covered with a blanket and she could smell food cooking on the fire. She sat up and stared. It was night and the two moons overhead, Iamar and Tomah, glowed between the treetops.

"Where are we? How did we get here?" The smell of roasting meat was enticing. "Where'd you get the meat?"

"Easy," Romarin said, kneeling down beside her. "You should've told me you got knocked in the head. That's what made you lose consciousness."

"And what would you have done?" she replied. "Not use the sword?"

Romarin chuckled. "I suppose." He glanced over at the meat roasting on the fire. "Are you hungry?"

"Very," she said. "But you haven't answered my questions. How did we get here?"

:How do you think you got here?

"Othala?" Kalena looked around and to her surprise, saw the dragon lying a few yards away, behind her.

:I knew when you had killed Torfar, Othala said, preening her scales. *:You do not kill such a great evil without a Fyr-dragon knowing about it.*

"She came to the lair and rescued us," Romarin said.

"But the fireworms?"

"They're not very friendly, but they do appreciate a good deed," Romarin said. "Torfar enslaved them – when we killed Torfar, we freed them. They let Othala carry us here."

"And they were appreciative of our efforts?"

Romarin shrugged.

:About as appreciative as those quarrelsome creatures can be. The fireworms thought they were being generous by not eating you, Othala said.

Kalena chuckled. "I would imagine."

"Do you feel all right?" he asked.

"I should be asking you that," she replied.

"I'm fine, though I've been wondering why only you could see Cahal and I couldn't," he said. "Although when Torfar attacked, for a split second, I saw Cahal standing before him with his hands outstretched."

"Cahal saved my life," Kalena said.

"I didn't know he knew magic."

"He said that changed when he entered the Hall of the Gods."

"Will we see him again?" Romarin asked.

Kalena shook her head. "While I was unconscious, he said goodbye."

"You saved my life – more than once, *Chi'lan*," Romarin said. "Can you stand up?"

"I think so," Kalena said, rising slowly and finding that she could stand without feeling dizzy. She turned to look at Romarin who had a very somber expression on his face. In his hands, he held *Fyren*. Her eyes widened as she realized the implication. "No," she whispered. "I told you, I don't want it…"

Romarin raised his hand to silence her objections. "But I do," he said. "Take your sword, *Chi'lan* Kalena of the Long Sword, Commander of the *Chi'lan*, the King's Champion."

Kalena met his gaze as she placed her hands on *Fyren*. The sword glowed with Romarin's power as she gripped it. "I accept it, my king."

For those interested in reading more about the World of *Chi'lan* please check out these other books by M. H. Bonham.

Timeline for the World of the Chi'lan

Lachlei – Dragon Moon Press, 2008, www.dragonmoonpress.com
(1500 years pass)

The King's Champion – Wolfsinger Publications, 2008, www.wolfsingerpubs.com

Serpent Singer and Other Stories – Yard Dog Press, 2008, www.yarddogpress.com

Prophecy of Swords – Yard Dog Press, 2005, www.yarddogpress.com

Runestone of Teiwas – Yard Dog Press 2007, www.yarddogpress.com

About the Author

M. H. Bonham or Maggie Bonham or Margaret H. Bonham (she does this regularly to confuse her publishers, but her fans figure it out) is a six-time award winning author of twenty-eight or so books, including her near award-winning novel, *Prophecy of Swords* (Yard Dog Press), *Runestone of Teiwas* (Yard Dog Press), *The King's Champion* (WolfSinger Publications), *Serpent Singer and Other Stories* (Yard Dog Press) and *Lachlei* (Dragon Moon Press). Maggie's SFF works include the award-winning *The Ultimate Weapon* (The Four Bubbas of the Apocalypse), *Cult of the Snagtar* (Flush Fiction), *Serendipity* (Houston, We've Got Bubbas), *Darkness Over All* (Small Bites, Tales of the Talisman), *Gunrunner* (More Sonic Stories, Tales of the Talisman), *A Storm Coming* (Tales of the Talisman), *Practice* (Kidvisions), *When the Vengeance is Gone* (A Time To…) and *Hellhounds* (Amazon.com).

In nonfiction, Maggie has 22 books on pets and pet care. She's written scads of articles that must run in the hundreds by now.

When Maggie isn't writing, she's racing sled dogs, climbing mountains, podcasting and practicing karate and ninjitsu somewhere in the wilds of the Rocky Mountains. She lives with her dashing husband, several sled dogs, four Malamutes (one named Haegl, who is named after the same black dragon in her stories, whom she swears is a dragon in a fur suit), and one very bold cat. Her current SFF projects include *Web of Wyrd*, the sequel to *Runestone of Teiwas*; *Outcasts of the Chi'lan*, the sequel to *Lachlei*; and *Samurai Son*, a Japanese-style fantasy, as well as other nonfiction and fiction projects. Maggie is the host of the *Sci Fi Traveling Road Show* podcast. Check it out at www.scifitravelingroadshow.com.

Visit Maggie's website at www.shadowhelm.net or www.lachlei.com, her blog at shadowhelm.livejournal.com, or email her at margaretbonham@aol.com. She has an email list for her fantasy books at ProphecyOfSwords-subscribe@yahoogroups.com – be sure to join up!

www.ingramcontent.com/pod-product-compliance
Lightning Source LLC
Chambersburg PA
CBHW052134170626
46812CB00004B/1403